Raven Manor

Ghostwolf Series, Book 1

T. L. RIFFEY

Publishing Coordinator – Sharon Kizziah-Holmes

Paperback-Press
an imprint of A & S Publishing
A & S Holmes, Inc.

ISBN -13: 978-1-951772-53-6

DEDICATION

Dedicated to those who understand that good and evil is all in the eye of the beholder.

Acknowledgments

Thanks to those who encourage me to keep writing.

CHAPTER 1

Detective John Hanlan drove through the wrought iron gate and pulled up behind the CSU and coroner's vans in the circular drive before the stone goliath. He had been pulled from his other cases by the Captain to handle this. She wanted it solved and quickly so she had called him. The captain had filled him in and recalled the original detectives. A good reputation could be a bad thing.

This place looked like a Gothic building from the fifteenth or sixteenth century. All spires, arches, and dark stone. He got out of his gray sedan and walked up to the uniform standing by the open front door.

The detective was a scarecrow of a man and his cheap ill-fitting suits didn't help, but the uniform at the door made him feel fat and old by comparison. The uniform was barely old enough to shave and Hanlan had hit the forty mark two years ago while the man was rail thin to Hanlan's lean build.

"Detective," the uniform said. "It's a bad one. CSU is still in there, the coroner's just waiting for you. Before they move the bodies"

Hanlan nodded and entered, pausing just inside. The front room was normal, just an entry area and sitting room to the one side. Another uniform stood at an open door just off the sitting area and two ME assistants stood with him, a stretcher beside them. He headed for the uniform who he recognized and had been told was the first on the scene.

"Jackson."

The uniform looked up. "Hanlan."

"So what happened?"

"Dan and I got the call about two hours ago. When we arrived the gate was already open as was the front door. We cleared the place. This door to the study and the bedroom door upstairs were locked. I thought I heard something inside this room so we kicked in the door." Jackson paused as he swallowed hard. "We called for back-up immediately."

"No forced entry?"

"Neither front nor back. There's a side door but it shows no sign of use for a while."

A young woman dressed in a pant suit leaned out the door. "I thought I heard your voice."

"Dr. Brennon." Hanlan gave her a nod. "What's the deal?"

"A male approximately sixty years old with

multiple sharp force trauma."

"As in stabbing?"

She shook her head. "As in bite and claw marks. His throat was ripped out as well as chunks of flesh. Preliminary cause of death is exsanguination."

Hanlan stepped into the room and stood stunned. The room was almost spotless. A body lay crumbled before the desk but none of the books that covered the walls had any blood splatter and there was only a small pool of blood by the body. "Where's the blood?"

Brennon gave him a grim smile. "My thoughts exactly. But I don't know."

"This is the only blood I found." The CSU tech looked up from his position near the body. "I did the perimeter but I'm waiting for the body to be removed before I do the desk area."

"Anything interesting besides no blood?" Hanlan asked the CSU tech.

"Nothing seems out of place on the bookshelves." He held up an evidence bag. "I did find this stuck in the window sill. It had to have snagged when the perp went out the window."

Hanlan took the bag and studied the short clump of course gray hair for a minute before handing it back to the tech. He moved over to the half-open window behind the desk and glanced outside at the bushes half covering the window. "You think he went out here?"

"The door was locked."

After another look at the bushes, Hanlan walked around the room. As the tech said nothing was disturb on the shelves and there was no blood splatter anywhere. "Thanks for letting me look before you took the body, Dr. Brennon."

She nodded, then said, "You want me to escort you to the bedroom?"

"Sure."

They both left the room and Brennon motioned for her assistants to enter before leading Hanlan to the staircase behind the back half wall. It was steep and made of the same stone as the outside of the house.

"You should read up on the history of this house," Brennon said as they went up the stairs. "It's pretty interesting."

"Does it have any bearing on this case?"

"This ain't the only strange murder that happened here."

Before he could say anything, they reached the landing and saw another uniform standing in front of an open door. Hanlan moved to the room and entered, staying just inside to look around. It was a surprisingly modern bedroom with a queen bed, a sitting area, and an en-suite. The woman's body lay flung across the bed and like the man downstairs the only blood visible was a small pool near the body.

"Same cause of death?" he asked Brennon.

"Yep."

A female CSU tech came out of the en-suite. "You gonna take the body now?" she asked Brennon.

"As soon as they're done with the one downstairs."

The tech nodded.

"Anything interesting?" Hanlan asked the tech.

"Besides the small blood pool?" The tech paused as she moved over to the bed and lifted a pillow. The stuffing came out of it through three large tears. "Just this so far."

"Knife, you think?" Hanlan asked.

"I don't know." the tech shrugged. "I'll know more once we get it back to the lab."

Hanlan nodded, then he and Brennon left the room. They headed back down the stairs. "You have any pearls of wisdom?"

"You know I don't speculate until after the autopsy." She paused her words. "But first blush the wounds look like an animal attack."

"What about the lack of spatter?"

Brennon shook her head as they stopped at the foot of the stair. "I don't know. It doesn't make sense that there's no blood except those little pools. The blood had to go somewhere."

"Send me your report as soon as you're done."

"Of course." She nodded to him, then headed toward the front door. Before she had taken too many steps, she stopped and looked at him over her shoulder. "You really do need to read the history of this place. Strange things have happened here before."

He waved his hand to her and as she continued walking, he turned and went back into the study. The crime scene tech was putting the items on top of the desk into evidence bags and Hanlan joined him. "Did you find a calendar or PDA?"

The tech handed him an evidence bag with a small desk calendar in it. "No PDA or any electronics. Not even a cell phone. Just the desk phone. You want me to bag up all this paperwork for you?" He gestured to the papers on the desk and in the half-open drawers. "I can drop it off at your desk when we get back."

"That would be great." He handed the calendar back to the tech and after one more glance around, he stepped back out of the room to find Jackson waiting for him. "Jackson. Was there something else?"

"This wasn't the first time we got a call to come here recently."

"Oh?"

"They had a visitor last week. When Dan and I arrived he was threatening them."

"I'd appreciate a copy of the report."

"You'll have it by tomorrow." Jackson nodded.

"Good."

Jackson said goodbye and headed for the front door while Hanlan went back upstairs, meeting the body on its way down. He waited for it to pass, then continued on up to the bedroom.

The tech was bagging the bedding when he entered. She nodded to him but didn't speak until she finished the bagging and tagging. "Was there something you needed, Detective?"

"No." He shook his head as he glanced around the room again. There was nothing out of place here either, like the study. Nothing disturbed but the area on the bed where the body had lain. He stepped out of the room and glanced down. His eyes focused on the fresh scars on the wooden floor.

The bedroom and study were carpeted but the entry and landing were wood. What looked like fresh claw marks marred the landing in front of bedroom and led to the wood stairs.

Hanlan went down the stairs with his eyes on the treads. He found a few marks on some of the steps but when he checked the entry he didn't find any. That was strange. If they had a dog there would be marks old and new in the entry. But Jackson hadn't mentioned anything about a dog and he would have if there had been one.

The tech from upstairs was coming down when Hanlan hailed her. "Wait a minute, would you?"

She stopped half-way down.

"Did you snap a picture of the marks on the landing in front of the bedroom door?"

"Yes."

"Good. May I have an extra copy of them?"

"Not a problem."

"Thank you." As she continued down he slipped into the study. "You'll be taking pictures of the ground outside the window, right?" He asked the tech there.

"CiCi did that before she went upstairs."

Hanlan ran his hand over the wooden sill but didn't feel any gouges nor did he see any when he studied the window. He definitely wanted to see those pictures. With a nod to the tech he walked out of the study into the entry.

The tech CiCi was headed up the stairs for another load of evidence but Hanlan barely registered her. His mind was cycling through what little he knew so far.

Both victims died of blood loss but only a small pool of blood was found near each. Their bodies showed marks from an animal attack. Nothing seemed to be taken or disturbed. There were fresh marks on the wood landing outside the one murder room but they supposedly didn't have a dog. And they had a visitor last week that threatened them.

He glanced at his watch. His shift had officially ended an hour ago and he knew most of the results wouldn't be in until morning. However he knew Dr. Brennon would have the autopsies done tonight. He could get dinner, then swing by and get the reports. She would probably even give him a verbal report and he could ask her about her comments regarding the house.

That decided he headed out of the manor into the evening light.

CHAPTER 2

The traffic was light tonight and Hanlan made good time across town. He had decided to eat at his favorite diner which was on the other side of town from the Morgue. Dr. Brennon should be done with at least one of the bodies.

He pulled into the back entrance of the hospital where the Morgue was located. There had been talk about adding on to the building where the new crime lab and new police station were located but the funding had never been allocated. So the Morgue had stayed here.

Dr. Brennon stood outside the Morgue entrance, a cigarette in her hand.

Hanlan parked and got out of his car. He joined Dr. Brennon at the door but didn't ask her for a cigarette. He had quit, but the urge was still there, though he hadn't smoked in years. Second hand smoke smelled good to him and was a compromise to his conscious. "Dr. Brennon."

"Hanlan."

"What's the verdict?"

"Exsanguination as I said."

"For both?"

"Yes." She nodded. "The throat was ripped out, then they bleed to death. The other wounds were postmortem."

"About those other wounds. You said it looked like an animal attack."

"What looks like claw marks and bites on the chest, thighs and shins. Don't quote me but the throat looks like it was ripped out by teeth. Very sharp teeth."

"A dog?"

"One very big dog, if it was, according to the diameter and force of the bites and placement of the claw marks."

He digested that for a moment as she finished her cigarette. "You got the reports done?"

"No." She shook her head. "Just finished the autopsies. Hadn't gotten to the paperwork yet. I'll send them your way first thing in the morning."

"Good." He paused. "What was that about strange things happening in that place?"

"Since you're not from around here, I figured you hadn't heard the stories about Raven Manor. It's almost an icon."

"I've been here almost ten years and I've never heard of it."

"You coppers tend to dismiss talk of the supernatural. Though the murders and disappearances are real enough."

He raised an eyebrow.

"God's Truth."

"Can you give me a brief summary?"

"I don't know about brief, but I can give you the highlights." She lit another cigarette to smoke while she talked. "The first disappearance of note was when it was being reconstructed in the 1800's. Three people disappeared: the chief engineer and his two helpers. No bodies, just vanished."

"Reconstructed?"

"Founding father Frank Alsena had it brought over from England." She took another drag from the cigarette. "Second disappearance was when they were wiring it for electricity. Two workers that time."

"I'm sensing a theme here."

"Gets better. The last disappearance happened when the new owners were remodeling. They both disappeared. That happened about fifteen years ago just before my guests bought it."

"And the murders? You mentioned murders."

"Just like a cop to go for the grizzly." She gave him a brief smile before becoming serious again. "A whole family was killed back in '69. Father, mother, and twin boys. All found in bed with their throats slit. House was torn apart, interior walls ripped open. Right mess. Most cops then put it down to drugs though there was nothing to suggest it. I read the autopsy reports. The wound tracks were strange, not any knife cut I've ever seen. And the M.E. at the time just said unknown weapon."

"1969?"

"Fall of '69." She nodded. "The place stood empty for a while afterwards."

"Their name."

"Duncan. John and Mary Duncan. The boys were John Junior and Samuel." She took another drag. "It was finally bought by one of those dot com entrepreneurs in the '80's. He was found bludgeoned just inside the door by the architect he was supposed to meet to discuss the remodeling. The M.E. listed the wounds as unusual. I saw the pictures and it looked like someone had punched him to death in the face with lead fists. After that, the place remained empty until the re-modelers I mentioned bought it."

"I need a date and name."

"Fall of 1986. Daniel Merser." She had finished her cigarette and grabbed the door handle. "The re-modelers were Dan and Joyce Cummings. I don't know if any of this will have any bearing on your investigation but I thought you should know the history of Raven Manor."

"It probably won't but information about a murder scene is always good."

"Good luck with your investigation. I'll have the reports to you tomorrow morning." She opened the door and disappeared inside.

Hanlan stared at the door, thinking. Tomorrow he was getting a new partner. A transfer from Vice. So a day in the bullpen might be in order. That decided he pulled out his phone and headed for his vehicle.

It was picked up just as he slid into his seat so he put it on speaker. "Jack."

"John. What can I do for you?"

"I need some case files pulled." He backed the car out and headed around the hospital. "I don't know if they'd be in the system as they are over fifty years old."

"Well, even if they were I'd still have the physical file."

"Which I prefer. I don't like computers."

A chuckle came from the speaker.

"Can you do it now?" The traffic was light and he wasn't in a real hurry, but he was half-way there.

"I gather you're on your way."

"Half-way."

"Okay. Shoot."

"Murder case. Fall of 1969. Duncan, John and Mary."

"Then you'll also be wanting the Merser file. If you're looking into the history of Raven Manor."

"Yes."

"I also got the missing persons file on the Cummings."

"I'd be interested in looking at it."

"Alright." There was noises of a chair rolling. "I'll have them ready when you get here." The phone went dead.

Hanlan had known Jack Reach since his first month in Homicide when he had arrived ten years ago. Jack was the guardian of files and evidence boxes. And he took his job very seriously. Nothing left his domain without a signature. Late nights had led to their meeting and they had hit it off from day one. Hanlan now considered him a good friend. Perhaps after he had read the files Jack would be open to questions.

The station building loomed up ahead. It was a five story high stone goliath with the crime lab in the two underground floors. A grant had been allocated to the city twenty years ago for a new crime lab and the Mayor had lobbied to combine the proposal of a new police station for this district with the allocated crime lab. Thus this building and a plaque in the main lobby.

He drove to the parking lot in the back and pulled into one of the slots marked "Detective". The file and property room--well, really several rooms-- was on the first floor so Hanlan got out of the car and jogged up the main steps. Once inside there were elevators and stairs to the right, a double door to the front, and a caged window with a cage door beside it to the left.

Nobody was at the caged window so Hanlan rang the bell on the desk top extending from the window.

An older man came up to the window, holding an evidence box. His salt and pepper hair and beard were neatly trimmed and his uniform crisp but loose on his mediumly built frame. "John."

"Jack." He gestured to the box. "That the files?"

"Yeah." He set the box on his side of the desk top before sliding a clipboard through the window slit. "Here."

Hanlan signed the clipboard where Jack had pointed.

"Stop by the bar Saturday morning." Jack

retrieved the clipboard and hung it below the window. "After five."

He knew that meant Jack would answer any questions he had about the files thus he nodded. Jack slid the files one by one through the slot so Hanlan could pick them up. They were thick files, at least four to six inches. "Thanks."

Jack just nodded.

Turning, Hanlan headed for the door. He would take them home tonight and review them. Or at least get a start. One wasn't supposed to take files home but some detective did anyway. Usually to make copies. Some cases never left the detective's mind, even when it was cold.

He jogged down the stairs and slid into the car. The files went into the passenger seat, then Hanlan started the car and backed out. His brain would probably not let him sleep tonight so he should at least get an overview of the files before he came to work in the morning. He headed toward his apartment.

Most detectives would dismiss everything but recent history of a crime scene like this. But one never knew what was connected and what wasn't. Ancient history might not be so ancient. Feuds lasted generations. Perhaps the victims were in the wrong place at the wrong time or maybe it was them that the killer was after. You had to sift carefully. A lot of the younger detectives dismissed things out of hand and missed precious clues, making twice the work when they had to rework the case.

The street he pulled into had a row of stone

houses, most with a basement apartment. This was an older neighborhood but the homeowners were yuppies. Converted basement meant money coming in that they could spend.

He drove around back of the one on the end and parked in his slot. When he had looked for apartments ten years ago he had lucked out. This basement apartment had just come up to rent the day he had looked at the basement apartment next door. He had been disappointed in the one he'd looked at and noticed the new sign being put up. The apartments were as different as night and day and he immediately paid the deposit, though he'd had to eat peanut butter and jelly sandwiches for a month.

Grabbing the files, he slid out of the sedan and headed to the stairway next to the main back stairs. There was a front and a back entrance while most had only one. He hurried down the stairs and ducked into the lighted covered entry. With a flick of the key, the door opened and Hanlan stepped inside.

Closing and locking the door behind him, he glanced around. The entryway was small with hooks beside the door holding his coats and an archway about six feet in front of him. Nothing seemed to be disturbed. He headed through the archway into the kitchen/living area. It took up half the space of the apartment. Moving on he stepped past the kitchen into the living room and headed toward the three doors on the wall to the left. He glanced in the archway leading to the front door to check for mail but didn't see any telltale whiteness.

As he past the coffee table he dropped the files there and continued on to the right hand door. It was his bedroom and he took off his suit jacket, hanging it on the bed's foot board as he moved to the open door leading to the bathroom between the two bedrooms.

He made a pit stop and washed his hands before going back into the main area through the bathroom door. Continuing on into the kitchen, he poured himself two fingers of whiskey before settling with it on the couch in the living room. Taking a sip of whiskey, he opened a file and began to read.

CHAPTER 3

Hanlan came in as usual through the back of the station to miss the chaos of the front desk and took the elevator to the fourth floor where the Homicide Division was. Major Case and Robbery shared the floor as well some of the Higher Ups that were banished from the rest of the Brass on the second floor.

He stepped off the elevator and headed down the hall toward the double wood doors that signified the Homicide Division's bullpen. This morning he had changed into one of his better suits as he wanted to make a good impression on his new partner. Good first impressions were essential to a good partnership.

Pushing open one of the wood doors, he stepped

inside and glanced to the left toward his area. Detectives were standing around his desk. He pushed his way past them to see a crime scene tech taking pictures. His desk was a mess. Everything in his drawers was scattered on the floor under his desk and files were a screw atop it. "What the hell happened here?"

"Don't know. It was found like this this morning," the tech said.

"Where were Howard and Ryn? They were on duty last night."

"Murder on Wilshore." came the Captain's voice as the African American woman stepped up to Hanlan. "They didn't return until five."

Hanlan grunted.

"Do you see anything missing?" she asked him. She was wearing a dress suit instead of her usual pant suit he noticed so she must have a meeting with the Brass today.

He glanced at his desk again, then shook his head. Everything seemed to be there, just not where it was supposed to be. Before he could say this to her, a messenger from the morgue came up to him and handed him a large envelope. The autopsy reports no doubt. He nodded to the messenger, then turned back to the Captain. "Everything seems to be here."

"Well, go through the files and make sure." She gestured to the top of his desk.

"Oh, I will," he promised.

The captain nodded and went back toward her office.

"That's it." The tech had gathered his stuff up

and was about ready to leave. "I'll keep you in the loop."

"Thank you." Hanlan watched the tech walk away, then laid the reports on his desk by the phone. He threw all the stuff from the floor into the big drawers. There would be time later to sort it. Pulling the chair up he sat and looked through the mess on his desk, sorting as he went.

Just as he got the last file together, someone stepped up to his desk and cleared their throat.

While the body and clothing were androgynous, the haircut was masculine. High and tight. And the cognac eyes were glittering like deep rubies in the pale face as he extended a slender hand. "Detective Hanlan, I'm Tom Canin."

Hanlan stood and shook his hand. Canin had a firm grip but he didn't try to break Hanlan's hand in a show of masculinity. Which gave him points in Hanlan's mind. "You already see Captain Gardner?"

"Yes and she already gave me the suit talk."

A smile touched Hanlan's face. Captain Gardner believed in professionalism and in her mind wearing a suit showed you were one. "Good. That's your desk." He gestured to the desk butted up to his. "Did she also tell you we caught a case yesterday evening?"

"Yes. A double homicide. But she said you'd give me the details."

Both men sat down at their desks.

Hanlan picked up the morgue reports and got them out of the envelope. "The victims are Mr. Anthony Graves and his wife Claire." He flipped through the reports as he spoke. "They were found yesterday evening around five by officers looking for intruders. It seems their security system went off at four-thirty and no one answered the call. So a Unit was dispatched."

"Those the autopsy reports?" Canin gestured toward the reports in Hanlan's hands.

"Yes." Hanlan slid them onto Canin's desk.

Before he could say anything else, the CSU tech from yesterday approached him with two large paper evidence bags. "I hear it was a good thing that I didn't drop these off last night," he said as he put the bags on Hanlan's desk.

"To tell the truth I had forgotten about them."

"I had too until this morning. I wanted to get them to you before I went home."

"Thanks."

The tech nodded and headed off.

"Do you want to read the reports or help me go through these?" Hanlan asked Canin. "This is the contents of Mr. Graves' desk."

Canin eyed the bags, then lifted the reports. "Read."

Hanlan set one of the bags on the floor, then upended the other bag onto his desk, shaking it to empty it. The empty bag went on the floor and he began sorting through the debris. Papers and envelopes went on a pile while pens and the like were dropped back into the bag. Once the debris was cleared, he looked through the papers and envelopes, sorting them into separate piles.

"Hand me the other bag," Canin said as he set the autopsy reports on the far corner of his desk.

"Catch." Hanlan tossed the heavy bag toward Canin who caught it just before it could hit him. "There should be a small desk calendar in that bag unless the lab kept it for some reason."

"Right."

Turning his attention back to his own desk, Hanlan flipped through the pile of bills. All were paid and up-to-date. Nothing unusual here. He put them back down and moved onto the next pile.

Correspondence. Several of the letters were from a lawyer named Brainard. They were vaguely threatening. It seems his client wanted to buy the Manor, but the Graves were refusing to sell and it wasn't sitting well with him or his client. Hanlan set those letters aside and continued reading but didn't find anything else probative.

The mail clerk laid an interoffice memo envelope on Hanlan's desk before moving on, causing Hanlan to look up at the clock. It was already 10.

Picking up the envelope, Hanlan leaned back in his chair and opened it. As he had suspected it was the incident report Jackson had promised him. He flipped through it, pausing briefly at the name of the perp before laying it back on his desk. His eyes went to his partner who was flipping backwards through the small desk calendar. "Canin?"

His partner flipped to the page his right hand was bookmarking and tapped it as he looked up. "Looks like he had an appointment the afternoon of the murder. But there is only a time and initials. I didn't see the initials anywhere else in the calendar."

"What about last Wednesday?"

Canin flipped back to the day, then shook his

head. "Different initials. J.B."

"John Brainard." Hanlan typed the name into his desk computer as he spoke. "He doesn't seem to have a Sheet."

"Do we know who he is?"

"A lawyer. It seems he was hired to get the Graves to sell their house to his client. At least that's what the letters say. Their tone is vaguely threatening and he had to be escorted from their property last Wednesday."

"Perhaps we should make a visit to Mr. Brainard."

"Just what I was thinking." Hanlan picked up his phone and dialed the number from the letters. "Yes, this is Detective Hanlan from the Alsena Police Department. I would like to make an appointment to speak with Mr. Brainard." He paused. "This afternoon if possible. It's important." A longer pause. "A murder investigation." Another pause. "That will be fine. Thank you."

As Hanlan hung up, Canin raised an eyebrow and asked, "He suddenly got a free moment?"

"Yes. Just after lunch." Hanlan drew open a drawer and pulled out a plastic evidence bag. After closing the drawer, he put the letters from Brainard inside the bag. Tossing the rest of the letters and bills inside the large bag on the floor, he straightened his desk before standing with the plastic bag in his hand. "Come on. Let me introduce you to one of our gatekeepers. That is unless there's something important in that bag."

Canin shook his head and dumped everything back into his large bag except the desk calendar which he put back in the plastic evidence bag he got it from. "Should we take this?" He shook the desk calendar bag.

"Yes." He turned and moved toward the double doors.

Standing Canin pushed in his chair, then followed Hanlan through the double doors towards the elevator.

Beside the elevator was a combination fax and copy machine and Hanlan headed straight for it.

"I thought we were going to evidence lockup." Canin looked at Hanlan questioningly.

"We will." Hanlan went on to make copies of the letters. "But I want to be able to confront Brainard with proof if he denies knowing the Graves."

"Ah."

Hanlan put the copies in a folder he got from under the fax/copy machine, then pressed the elevator button. Everything he knew so far was percolating in his brain. He didn't have a theory just yet but he was sure something would come to him with the right stimulus. Meanwhile he had a new partner to break in.

The elevator arrived and they stepped in, the front set of doors closing behind them. Hanlan pressed the button, then looked over at Canin. "The head cheese of the evidence lockup is Jack Reach but he works nights. He knows everything about the evidence lockup rooms. You need to stay on his good side. Sgt. Dan is the day guy. He's real finicky about paperwork."

"I'll remember that."

A minute later the back doors opened and they

stepped into the back entry. Hanlan headed for the caged window and the younger dark-haired man in a uniform standing on the other side.

"Hey, Sgt. Dan." Hanlan laid his evidence bag on the desk top and motioned for Canin to lay his there too. "How you doing today?"

"Fair." Sgt. Dan pulled a clipboard from below the desk and slid it through the slit. "I heard you drew the double murder at Raven Manor."

"Yep." Hanlan filled out the paper quickly, then slid it back to Dan. "Didn't know if you met my new partner yet."

"Hadn't." Dan accepted the two bags through the slit, then looked at Canin. "I'm Sgt. Jim Daniels. Everyone calls me Sgt. Dan."

"Detective Tom Canin."

Sgt. Dan gave him a nod, then looked at Hanlan. "Anything else you need, Detective?"

"Not right now, Sgt. Dan. See you later." Hanlan turned away, but instead of heading for the elevator he headed for the back door. "Let's get some lunch. Then we can see Brainard."

"Alright." Canin fell into step with Hanlan and followed him into the parking lot. "I see where he got that nickname. Sgt. Dan does look like the actor who played in that movie."

"It's more than that. He has an artificial leg, a bi-product of a shooting eight years ago. He told them he was too young to retire so they offered him that job. One of the clerks had retired so there was an opening. Otherwise he'd would have been retired on disability."

They got into Hanlan's car and he backed out

before driving around the building. He'd take Canin to the nearby cop diner Joey's, a familiar place, and learn a bit more about him than what his jacket said.

Then they would beard Mr. Brainard in his den.

26

CHAPTER 4

Mr. Brainard's office was in an older three-story building in an older part of Alsena called Alsena Heights. A little out of their district but since this was only supposed to be an interview, Hanlan decided not to call anyone. He hoped it wouldn't come back to bite him in the ass.

They entered the building and bypassed the empty desk. The legend said his office was on the second floor so they took the elevator up. A sign pointed them to the left and a glass door with Brainard's name on it.

Canin opened the door and they both strode in.

A high desk sat a few feet in front of them while to the right was a waiting area. Short hallways lead off to the left and right to closed doors. Everything was worn but in good condition and gave off the feeling of comfort instead of money.

"Can I help you?" Eyes peered over the desk.

They stepped forward. An older woman sat at the desk. Obviously the receptionist/secretary.

"We're here to see Mr. Brainard. I'm Detective Hanlan."

"Oh, of course." She tapped a button on her desk phone. "Sir, the detectives are here."

"Send them in."

The woman pointed them to the door at the end of the right hallway. "That's his office."

"Thank you." Hanlan gave her a nod, then both of them headed for the door. He tapped it once then opened it and went inside with Canin. The door closed behind them as they moved further inside the office.

The office was a combination office and conference room. A big oval table and chairs took up one side while a large wooden desk with wing back chairs in front of it took up the other. A middle-aged man in a nice dark suit stood up from the desk and gestured to the two chairs.

"Please sit down. Cynthia said you wanted to talk to be about a murder investigation." Brainard's demeanor was calm, but his eyes were wary.

All three sat and Hanlan nodded. "Yes. Mr. and Mrs. Graves were killed yesterday afternoon."

"I see."

The lawyer looked thoughtful but his eyes remained wary. Hanlan allowed the silence to grown for a bit while he studied the man. Brainard's face was careworn like the décor giving one a sense of comfort which probably served the lawyer well, lending him a trustworthiness to his clients. Whether he truly was was another matter.

Hanlan noticed his partner was staring at Brainard rather intensely. Had he noticed something? He would have to ask later. "You had an argument with the deceased," he told the lawyer. "where you threatened them."

"To make their lives miserable, not kill them."

"You promised to 'make them wish they were dead', I believe you said." Hanlan waved the file in his hand. "And these letters sound threatening to me."

"They were being unreasonable."

"Because they didn't want to sell their house?"

"It was a very generous offer."

"As would be your fee if you succeeded, no doubt."

Brainard merely stared at him.

"We need to get in touch with your client," Canin spoke up. "If you would be so kind as to give us their name and address we will leave you to your work."

"I can't do that. Client/attorney privilege. However if you give me your card I will pass it on to my client."

"And I can have you up on obstruction charges," Hanlan told him. "Maybe a few days in holding might soften you up."

"I'd be out in a day at the most. Now, gentlemen." He stood. "I have a meeting in a few minutes. So I will have to bid you to leave."

"Give him your card, Hanlan," Canin said as

they both stood. "We can talk to the Captain."

Hanlan handed Brainard a card from his jacket pocket. "We'll be back," he warned.

Brainard inclined his head to him but didn't speak.

"By the way, where were you yesterday afternoon?" Hanlan asked from the doorway.

"Here. From two until six."

Canin and Hanlan exited the office then and walked toward the front desk.

A young woman was sitting in the waiting area and looked up when they stopped to speak to the receptionist/secretary. Hanlan noted that she was wearing high quality clothes and had a fancy haircut but dismissed her from his mind as he turned his attention back to the business at hand.

"Mr. Brainard said he was here yesterday from two until six. Can you verify that?"

"Yes." The receptionist/secretary nodded. "He came back from a late lunch at just before two and had two appointments. I left at 5:30 pm. and he was still in the office with his last appointment."

"Thank you, Ms..." Hanlan trailed off for her to speak.

"Sharp. Helen Sharp."

"Ms. Sharp. Can you give us the names associated with those appointments?"

"Now, Detective, you know I can't do that." She waved a finger at him. "I've worked for Mr. Brainard for over ten years and I know what I can and can't do legally."

Brainard came out of his office just then and frowned when he saw them at the desk. "Why are you still here? Are you harassing my secretary?"

"Actually they were verifying your alibi," the young woman said in a totally unexpected smokey voice from the waiting area. She rose gracefully to her feet, her cognac colored eyes on Canin.

Who Hanlan just notice was tense as a spring, almost as if he was expecting an attack. "And you are?"

"Julia Lupo," the woman said as Brainard opened his mouth.

"As in Lupo Medical?"

She inclined her head.

"No offense, but why are you here? You're a billion dollar company and can afford a better attorney."

"Personal matter."

Before she could say anything more, Brainard spoke up. "That's enough. You don't have the right to question my client. Please leave."

"We will be back." Canin said, his own cognac eyes on Lupo.

Lupo tilted her head to Canin as Brainard repeated, "Please leave."

Hanlan and Canin nodded to Brainard, then left the office and headed for the elevator.

"What was that about?" Hanlan asked Canin.

"What do you mean?"

At the elevator Hanlan turned and looked at Canin. "That stare off between you and Ms. Lupo."

"I don't know what you mean." Canin's face was blank of expression.

"Don't." Hanlan met Canin's eyes. He absently noted they were the same color as Lupo's but dismissed it for now as he had more important things on his mind. "I am a Detective and a good one at that."

Canin remained silent.

Hanlan hit the elevator button and the doors opened. He whirled and stepped inside. "I thought we were partners."

"We are," Canin said with a sigh as he joined him in the elevator.

"Then talk to me."

The doors closed and Hanlan hit the button for the first floor.

"I can't." Canin paused. "At least not yet. But I think Ms. Lupo is the interested party for Raven Manor."

"So do I." Hanlan paused as he looked at Canin. "I'll let you have your secrets for now but if they effect this case I need to know them."

Canin inclined his head in acknowledgment.

They arrived on the first floor and the doors opened. The desk was still empty and they barely gave it a glance when they walked by toward the front door.

"We'll have to talk to the Captain about getting the name of his client and his official alibi."

"Can't we just go by the local precinct first?" Canin asked as they headed down the street to where they parked the car. "Since we're here?"

"We have to go through the proper channels." Hanlan shook his head. "We might already get a reaming for this visit."

"What for? We just talked with him."

"Still out of our district. Our station may house

the main Brass but it don't give us the right to step on other precincts' toes. At least so I've been told," he added with humor in his voice. It was ironic that he was lecturing the newbie on this. He broke that 'rule' a lot. Wherever the investigation leads him is where he went, no matter where he had to go.

Canin grunted but didn't comment.

The two of them made it to the car and slid inside. Hanlan started the car and pulled out into the street.

They would check in with the lab when they got back to see if anything was done yet, then they would have to talk to the Captain. Brainard may not have done the deed, but Hanlan felt he was involved somehow. And Ms. Lupo needed checking on. Something just wasn't right there.

Hanlan turned left and headed toward his station. He glanced over at Canin who was staring out the window.

At lunch Canin had been very general about his life. Hanlan had learned very little personal details about his new partner but then he hadn't given out much of his own. He had experienced good and bad partnerships as well as working alone. He preferred a partner. And he was getting a good vibe from Canin. But he was holding something back. Hanlan could sense it. Hopefully, Canin would trust him and tell him. Secrets between partners could be deadly.

CHAPTER 5

Captain Gardner saw them right away when they returned to the station. She sat behind her old metal desk quietly, her whole attention on them as they told her what they had so far. When they finished she stared thoughtfully at the door behind them and leaned forward, resting her elbows on the desk. "Are any of the other reports in besides the autopsies yet?"

"I was going to call down and see," Hanlan told her. "But nothing was on my desk."

"I'll call the other precinct and get the ball rolling over there." She looked at him. "You know you should have come to me before you went to interview him."

Hanlan inclined his head in acknowledgment.

She stared at him for a minute, then gestured dismissively. "Get back out there and see if you can find some other leads."

"Thank you, Captain." Hanlan turned and led his partner back to their desks. He slid into his chair and reached into his inbox for the file on top. Checking the tab, he opened the file and flipped through it rapidly.

Canin stood for a moment then sat in his own chair. "What's that?"

"Neighbor statements." Hanlan tossed the file onto his desk. "Nobody witnessed anything. Two hundred feet apart and no one saw or heard anything."

"Picture the neighborhood for me."

"English Manor like homes enclosed in stonewalls with wrought iron gates. Both sides of the street. Raven Manor has a bit more space around and behind it then the others."

"Affluent neighborhood."

"At least those that aspire. As you know the truly affluent live in one of Towers. Their every whim satisfied."

Canin made a face.

Hanlan was just grateful he didn't work that area and wouldn't. Everyone told him he didn't have a political bone in his body and he was glad. Babysitting spoiled brats was not what he joined the Force for.

"When we briefed the Captain you said Graves was a retired Professor." Canin paused as Hanlan nodded. "What did he teach that he could afford Raven Manor?"

"He had been the Chair of the Archaeology Department for twenty years was what I was told when I was briefed and recently retired. But they bought the Manor fifteen years ago after the disappearance of the previous owners."

Canin raised an eyebrow.

"Gets better. There's been two other strange murders that happened in that place."

"Recent?"

"No." Hanlan shook his head. "Both are still open cases though. I'll bring the files in tomorrow after I finish them tonight."

"You took them home?"

"Yeah." Hanlan shrugged. "I wasn't going to be sleeping much anyway."

Canin grunted.

Hanlan picked up the phone and dialed the Lab. "This is Detective Hanlan," he said when they picked up. "Are any results in for the Graves Case yet?" He paused. "Yes, I'll hold."

Both leaned back in their chairs as they waited. Canin grabbed the autopsy reports and flipped through them again as the minutes ticked by.

"Yes, I'm still here." Hanlan straightened and nodded as he listened. "Okay. Thank you," he said before hanging up the phone.

"Well?" Canin threw the reports back on his desk.

"They got an identification on the hair found stuck in the study window. Canis Lupus. Wolf hair."

"Hmm." Canin looked thoughtful. "Anything else?"

"They're sending up the pictures of the crime scenes." He paused as a lab rat appeared at his desk with two big envelopes. "Speak of the devil."

"Sorry they're late, Detective," the lab rat said. "But we had trouble with the printer."

Hanlan grabbed the envelopes and set them down on his desk before waving a dismissive hand. "It's okay."

The lab rat bobbed his head and scurried away.

"Here." Hanlan threw both of the envelopes toward Canin. "Familiarize yourself with the crime scenes."

Canin managed to catch the envelopes and set them on his desk. He opened one and pulled out the photos. A soft whistle made it past his teeth.

"Yeah." Hanlan didn't need the photos to picture the scenes again. It was almost burned into his mind. The inherent violence had seared through him.

"Wait. Where's all the blood?"

Hanlan shrugged.

"Hmm." Canin finished looking through the photos, then slipped them back into their envelope before opening the other envelope. He flipped through those pictures, pausing here and there, before returning them back to their envelope. "Definitely strange."

"Any observations?"

"No sign of forced entry?"

"None."

"Then the J.L. that he had an appointment with is definitely a person of interest." Canin tilted his head. "I suppose being the newbie I get to do all the legwork."

"A lot of guys do that, but not me." Hanlan typed in Julia Lupo's name into his computer. He was attached to several data bases, thanks to his last partner. "A partnership is just that, a partnership. That being said, I do have seniority."

Canin nodded.

"So go fetch the printouts, would you?"

Rolling his eyes, Canin stood, then headed for the printer by the front doors.

Hanlan closed out of the search engine and leaned back in his chair. There hadn't been much about Julia Lupo's private life in what he had found, though her company was splashed all over the news almost every day. There was an air of mystery surrounding her that seemed a bit sinister to Hanlan, not enticing as it did to other people. She had secrets. And he didn't think they were nice secrets either.

His partner returned just then, bringing him out of his thoughts.

"Not much here." Canin was holding two papers out to Hanlan. "I thought there'd be more."

"There's plenty about the company." Hanlan took the pages. "But little about Ms. Lupo herself."

"Something to hide?" Canin sat in his chair and slouched.

"Maybe." He'd been ignoring the noise of the busy bullpen—well, both of them had—but now he let himself sink into the ebb and flow. It helped to clear his mind. Wisps of conversations. Detectives walking by. Phones ringing.

Speak of the devil. His own phone rang. He

answered it with "Hanlan."

Canin straightened in his chair and looked at Hanlan when Hanlan hung up the phone a few minutes later. "Well?"

"That was the Captain. The detectives served Brainard while they were getting his alibi. Julia Lupo is the client interested in Raven Manor."

"Want to bet she's the J.L. listed on the calendar too?"

"Gives us a reason to question her anyway." Hanlan looked up her phone number on the pages and dialed. "Hmm. Yes, this is Detective Hanlan of the Alsena Police Department. We met earlier today at Brainard's office." He paused. "Yes. I was wondering if you could come in and answer a few questions." Another pause. "That would be fine." He paused again. "I'll see you then, Ms. Lupo. Goodbye."

Canin raised an eyebrow at Hanlan as he hung up the phone.

"Whether Brainard will be with her, I don't know but she said she'd be in tomorrow morning at nine. She has an appointment this afternoon."

"This evening she should say." His partner glanced at the clock. "It's almost four."

Hanlan shrugged.

"Here." Canin handed over a file. "While you were daydreaming, I started to put together the case file."

"I wasn't daydreaming I was thinking." Hanlan set the file on his desk and tapped it. "There's a lot of unusual elements to this case."

Canin started typing on his computer as he gave

Hanlan a nod. "True. What were you thinking about?"

"An old Roma story my great grandmother told me when I was little."

"Your great grandmother was Roma?" Canin's head had jerked up and he was staring at Hanlan.

"Yes, from Romania." Hanlan was staring at the case file so he missed the intense stare though he had caught the head jerk out of the corner of his eye. "Some of the elements from the case reminded me of the story and I was trying to recall what she said." He shook his head as he brought his mind back to the present. "Anyway, we can ask Ms. Lupo if she has any wolves as pets."

Canin turned back to his computer and started typing again. "Like she'd tell us the truth on that."

Hanlan shrugged and slid the two pages on Julia Lupo in the case file. Looked like Canin was filing out the initial case report to add to the case file so he leaned back in his chair. He knew he should be writing up the daily report but he didn't want to. There was a lot on his mind with this case.

"There." Canin got up and disappeared toward the printer. He was back moments later and handed the report to Hanlan. "That's the initial. I also did the daily notes."

"Good. I was contemplating whether I wanted to do it."

"Well, now you don't have to." Canin sat and leaned back in his chair as Hanlan slid the report into the case file. "You think we should talk to the University?"

"No. But we will have to visit some of his

friends. We can't just focus on Brainard and Lupo."

"Have the bodies been released yet? I didn't see that in the reports."

"The M.E. usually holds on to them for at least forty-eight hours. So the funeral will probably be day after tomorrow. We can catch up with most of the Graves' friends there."

Canin nodded.

Hanlan grabbed the autopsy reports and flipped open Mr. Graves'. He ran his finger down the one page, then picked up his phone. After dialing the number he found, he closed the report and laid them on the desk, holding the phone to his ear with his shoulder until he could hold it with his hand.

"Who?" Canin mouthed.

Holding up a finger, Hanlan spoke. "Yes. This is Detective Hanlan with the Alsena Police Department. I'd like to make an appointment to speak with Mr. Stephan Shaw tomorrow afternoon regarding his late clients the Graves." He paused. "That will be fine. Thank you."

"And who is Mr. Stephan Shaw?" Canin asked as Hanlan hung up the phone.

"The Graves' lawyer. And the one who made the ID."

Two detectives that were moving past them toward the door stopped and the older one asked, "Did I hear you say Shaw?"

Hanlan twisted in his chair to look at them. "Yes, Stephan Shaw."

"He any relation to Robert Shaw the lawyer?"

"Son, I think. Why?"

"We just got called to his office. Robert Shaw

was found dead half an hour ago."

42

CHAPTER 6

Shaw Consulting was not far from the station in a newly renovated building. Hanlan noted that their front lobby desk was attended by a uniformed guard so maybe they would catch a break on the perp.

He and Canin had followed the other detectives here to see if this might pertain to their murders. Howell and Denegue were agreeable so Hanlan wasn't worried about stepping on their toes. If this murder was related to the Graves' then either he and Canin would take the case or they would work with Howell and Denegue.

They all went up to the sixth floor by the public elevator. CSU had cleared the public elevator but were still working on the private. The doors slid open to reveal a carpeted area with glass doors etched with the firm's name. Shaw Consulting had the whole floor.

Uniforms and CSU techs roamed the area. The detectives followed the uniform that had rode the elevator with them to an office in the back.

The office looked like a rich man's study. There was a seating area around what looked like an electric fireplace to the left and a fancy wooden desk with wing back chairs facing it to the right. Wood paneling covered the walls as did oil paintings.

Hanlan felt uncomfortable in such opulence but pushed that aside as he stepped toward the desk beside which the body lay. There was little blood but he could see that the throat was ripped out like the Graves'.

"I didn't expect to see you here, Hanlan," Dr. Brennon said from her position kneeling beside the body. "Though I should have, I suppose."

"Then it is identical to the Graves'?" He asked her.

"I'd have to do a full autopsy to know for sure but the preliminary observation seems to point that way, yes." She straightened from the body. "When you'll are done I'll have my people take the body."

All four of the detectives nodded to her as she left. While Howell and Deneque looked at the body Hanlan glanced at the papers on the desk and did a double take. He pointed out the file name to Canin but didn't say anything to the other two detectives.

Canin gave a small nod of acknowledgment.

Howell and Deneque straightened and turned

toward Hanlan. "You taking over?"

"If the autopsy confirms manner and cause of death the same as the Graves'" Hanlan nodded. "Until then you can run with it if you want."

Both of the other detectives shook their heads and Howell spoke again. "Nah. We've got plenty on our plate already."

"The Olsen case?"

"And I got Court this week." Howell made a face.

"Okay. Get out of here." Hanlan gave a wave toward the door. "We'll take it from here."

Howell and Deneque nodded and hurried out the door, nearly running over the CSU tech entering behind the stretcher and the morgue assistants.

"Did you already take pictures?" Hanlan asked the tech as the assistants knelt by the body.

"Yes." The tech nodded. "I'm just going to check the area over again after Dr. Brennon's people take the body."

"So you got pictures of the desk and what's on it?"

"Yes, but the son wouldn't let us take anything off the desk." The tech knelt as the assistants lifted the now body bag encased corpse onto the stretcher. "But I made sure I got pictures of everything."

"Good." Hanlan paused as the stretcher was wheeled out. "His son was here?"

"Still is. You probably passed him coming in."

"All right. Thank you." Hanlan did vaguely recall a young man in a suit as they were being led here. He motioned to Canin and they left the office, heading for the firm's lobby.

Sitting in one of the cushy chairs was a dark-haired man holding his head over his lap. He looked up as Hanlan and Canin approached him. His dark eyes were red-rimmed but dry.

"Mr. Shaw?"

"Yes."

"I'm Detective Hanlan and this is my partner Detective Canin. Sorry for your loss."

Shaw nodded, then frowned. "Hanlan. Don't I have an appointment with you tomorrow?"

"Yes. Why did your father have the Graves' file on his desk? I thought you were their attorney."

"I am. But Father handles--handled most of the probates."

"Hmm. Can you tell me what happened?"

"Father had called me and told me to stop by before I went home as something had come up about the Graves' probate. He said he was meeting with someone shortly to clear it up he hoped, but in any case, he wanted to see me. So when I was ready to leave, I headed to his office. The door was open and I stepped in... That's when I saw him."

"You didn't see or hear anything?"

"My office is toward the front and to the right. Marie, my secretary, didn't mention anything either before she left just after five."

"We'll need her name and phone number as well as the receptionist's."

"Of course." He stood and went over to the reception desk. Grabbing a pen and a pad, he scribbled the information down before holding out the paper toward Canin who had followed him to the desk. "Here."

Canin took the paper and glanced at it, then slipped it into his jacket pocket.

"We still need to come by tomorrow and ask you about the Graves'," Hanlan told Shaw.

"I really can't tell you much. Attorney/client privilege still applies."

"They're dead. They're not going to sue you." Canin frowned at him.

Shaw shrugged.

"I'll see about a subpoena." Hanlan gestured for Canin to head toward the door. "Come on. We need to get back to the station."

Both detectives moved toward the glass doors. Most of the CSIs and officers had left but a few were still moving about. The detectives slipped past the activity and got on the elevator without being stopped which Hanlan took as a victory. They rode down to the building lobby and Hanlan headed straight to the guard desk as soon as the elevator doors opened.

"I'm Detective Hanlan and this is my partner Detective Canin. When did you come on duty?" he asked the uniformed guard seated at the desk.

"I'm Tom Hastings. I get here a little before three. We don't actually check anyone in, you know. We're just here in case we're needed to escort people from the premises or to keep people out."

"But you see everyone that comes in or out."

"Yes." Hastings nodded at Hanlan. "And we have video surveillance of the doors and lobby."

"We need a copy of today's tape. Or at least of the last three hours."

"I thought you might." Another uniformed man

joined them at the desk, holding a VHS tape. "The security system is old school but it gets the job done. I'm the day supervisor Daniel Harvey." He held out the tape to Hanlan. "That's from three until you showed up. Hope it helps."

"Thanks." Hanlan took the tape gratefully. They wouldn't have to fight the company for the footage, causing delays.

Harvey nodded and headed toward a door by the public elevator. Obviously on the way back to the security room.

Hanlan and Canin hurried outside to the car and sped to the station once they got inside. They took the back elevator to the fourth floor but instead of going in the bullpen they headed for the conference room where they knew they would find a VCR. The Lab could run off a DVD from the tape but they were in a hurry to see the video.

The conference room was small but cozy with a TV cabinet at the front of the room. Canin planted his butt on the oval table while Hanlan opened the TV cabinet. Hanlan then slipped in the tape, grabbing the remote as he stepped back. An image of the lobby door flickered to life on the TV screen and Hanlan fast forwarded until a woman entered.

Her face was blurred but the clothes were unmistakable. Hanlan froze the image and squinted at the face but it didn't clear up.

"She was wearing those clothes at Brainard's."

"But the face is too blurry," Canin objected. "Any good lawyer could argue that."

"Maybe the techs can clear it up." Hanlan looked at the image one more time then shut the video off.

He retrieved the tape and headed toward the door. "Let's see if the Captain's still here. And turn this tape in to CSU."

Canin slid off the table and followed Hanlan out.

They met the Captain in the hallway, just leaving the bullpen. She stopped, turned around and led them back to her office.

"Okay. What's up?" She leaned against her desk, her eyes on Hanlan.

"First. Canin, can you take this to the Lab, then get started on the paperwork? I'll join you as soon as I'm done updating the Captain."

"Sure." Canin took the tape from Hanlan, then disappeared out the office door.

Hanlan took a deep breath, then filled the Captain in on Shaw's murder. He included the file on Shaw's desk as well as what they had just seen on the tape.

"Canin's right. We can't arrest her on that. However, we can have her come in for questioning."

"She's already coming in tomorrow morning about the Graves'."

"Excellent. Two birds with one stone." She straightened. "I'll see about the subpoena in the morning while you question Ms. Lupo."

"Thank you, Captain."

"Now I need to get home before my husband sends a search party for me. I was supposed to be home an hour ago."

"See you in the morning, Captain." Hanlan left the office and headed for his desk. Canin was at his own desk, typing on the computer, and Hanlan slumped into his chair. "The tape downstairs?"

"Yep. I'm doing the initial report if you want to do the notes." He handed Hanlan a piece of paper. "That's the receptionist's and secretary's numbers."

Hanlan glanced at the paper, then put it down on his desk before he started working on his own computer. He put down just the bare facts, no speculation, when he did the notes. Other detectives said it might as well be a report instead of notes of one's thoughts on a case. Hanlan liked to keep his thoughts in his head where they won't get him in trouble.

"There." Canin stood and retrieved the report from the printer. He shoved it into a folder and laid it on his desk. "I'm done."

Closing out the notes, Hanlan leaned back in his chair. "So am I. You want to get a beer?"

"I got plans." Canin shook his head. "A rain check?"

"Sure."

"See you in the morning." Canin gave Hanlan a little wave and headed out.

Hanlan glanced at the clock. He could pick something up at Chickies' on the way home. There was still a lot to go through on the past two murders. Looked like he wasn't going to be getting much sleep tonight either, though for a different reason.

Everything was linked together. He could sense that in his gut but nothing solid bore that out. Shaw's murder didn't feel the same as the Graves', though they looked physically identical. Something was missing.

Sitting here wasn't helping any. So he stood and headed out. He could do his brooding at home.

CHAPTER 7

Dreams had disturbed what little sleep Hanlan had gotten. He had finished the files around 1 a.m. but hadn't gotten to sleep until after three. His thoughts had kept circling until pure exhaustion had taken over. However images of blood-covered wolves attacking him had kept him from really sleeping.

When his alarm had gone off he had been almost grateful. He had mainlined coffee and grabbed the files of other murders at Raven Manor before leaving for the station. Drive-thru had netted him a breakfast burrito and he had eaten it on the way.

Hanlan took the back elevator up to the fourth floor as usual then headed toward the bullpen. The coffee and the burrito had done its job and he was feeling ready to work.

A suit-clad Canin was at his desk when Hanlan entered and he made his way over to his own desk. He set the murder files on Canin's desk before sitting in his chair. "Those are the files of the other murders that had happened at the Manor. I also got a file on the last disappearance, but I didn't bring it." He wanted to go over it again. There was something that was setting his gut off about it.

Grabbing the top one, Canin pulled the file closer then opened it. He flipped through the file, then closed it and grabbed the other. After flipping through it, he closed that file and set both of them to the side. "You want to give me the short version?"

"1969. The Duncan family. Husband, wife, and twin boys. Throats slit. All found in their beds. House torn apart. Including the walls. It was thought to be drug related though no evidence of them were found. The M.E. couldn't identify the weapon used."

"But it was the same for all of them?"

"Yes." Hanlan nodded. "No forced entry. No extra fingerprints. No unusual cars seen in the days leading up to the murders."

"So the case went cold pretty fast."

"Yep."

"I gather there was blood or you would have mentioned that tidbit."

"Yep." Hanlan smiled.

"What about the second murder?"

"1986. Daniel Merser. A dotcom businessman. Beaten to death. With fists. According to the M.E. report first his body, then his face was beaten severely, to the point he had to be identified by dental records."

"Did you say fists?" Canin looked at him sharply.

"Yep. More damage to the house was noted, though this time to the outside and yard."

"So, both murders entailed a search."

"Yep."

Canin gave him an irritated look.

Hanlan laughed. He didn't know why but he liked getting a rise out of his partner.

The Captain came up to Hanlan's desk and handed him an envelope. "Your subpoena."

"How'd you get it so early?" Hanlan took the subpoena and put it in his jacket's left inner pocket.

"Judge Peterson."

"He's always in his chambers by 7a.m.," Hanlan said at Canin's raised eyebrow.

"Ms. Lupo's coming in at nine?" The Captain asked.

"Yes." Hanlan nodded. "Did you want to observe?"

"I thought I would."

"Alright." Hanlan nodded again. "I don't know if she's bringing Brainard."

"It'd be smart for her to. Either way you know what to do."

"Yes, Ma'am." He watched her walk away, then looked at Canin. "I'm usually the bad cop. Fits me fine. But if you want to play worse cop..." Hanlan shrugged. "However I prefer to play it straight this time."

"Fine by me. I had enough games with Vice."

Hanlan nodded. His phone rang just then and he picked it up. "Hanlan." A pause. "Yes, I'm expecting her. Bring her up to Interview Room 2, if you would. Thank you."

"She's early," Canin commented as Hanlan hung up the phone.

"To throw us off our game maybe." Hanlan stood. "I'll tell the Captain."

Before he could take more than a few steps toward her office, the Captain approached him. "I saw you stand up. She here?"

"Yes. One of the officers will bring her to Interview Room 2."

"Good. I'll be in Observation."

Hanlan nodded, then headed toward the back of the bullpen where the Interview Rooms were. The rooms were there to help trap suspects in case they tried to run.

Canin caught up to him before Hanlan got more than a few steps and walked beside him to the corridor at the back.

Doors lined that short corridor and they headed to the one marked 'Interview 2'. Hanlan opened the door and motioned Canin to enter, then followed the man inside. A table with four chairs occupied the center of the small room and a camera was set above the mirror that took up half of the one wall. Both detectives sat in the chairs with their backs to the mirror.

Moments later a uniform escorted Lupo into the room. She was wearing a black skirt and jacket with a white silk blouse. Her hair was more wild today but was still styled.

Both detectives stood and Hanlan gestured to a chair. "Good morning, Ms. Lupo. Would you please sit down?"

"Detectives." Lupo inclined her head to them, then sat primly in one of the chairs as the uniformed officer left.

The detectives sat as Hanlan spoke again. "Thank you for coming in to speak with us. But I'm surprised Mr. Brainard isn't with you."

"I'm not under arrest, am I?"

"No. We just have some questions."

"Then why would I need a lawyer?" She raised an eyebrow as she looked at him. "Now ask your questions, Detective."

"Did you have a meeting with Mr. Graves two days ago in the afternoon?"

"Yes."

"When did you leave?"

"About 2:30 pm., I believe. I wasn't there long."

"Where did you go after you left the Manor?"

"To my apartment. I stayed in all night."

"Is there anyone that can corroborate that?"

"I was alone. However the apartment building does have cameras on the doors."

"We'll check them out."

"Do that."

Hanlan paused in his questioning. She had answered every question calmly and straight forward but with no extra information. Let's see if she would do the same when he switched to Shaw. "You told me you had an appointment yesterday afternoon. Was it with Mr. Robert Shaw by any chance?"

"Why would you ask that?"

"Someone who looked remarkably like you entered his building a little over an hour before he was found dead."

"That sounds a bit like an accusation." She stood. "Since I'm not under arrest I think I will leave now."

"Before you go, will you answer one last question?" Canin spoke up.

Her cognac eyes went to Canin as she raised an eyebrow.

"Why are you interested in Raven Manor?" His own cognac eyes watching her.

"Ancestral home." She turned and headed for the door. "If you want to talk to me again about this nonsense contact Mr. Brainard."

Both detectives watched her leave.

According to the dates and information on his unofficial background check, Hanlan knew she had hired Brainard after she had become C.E.O. of Lupo Medical last month. If her family had known the Manor was their ancestral home why hadn't they bought it back in 2005? Was that knowledge newly acquired?

"What do you think?" Canin asked him, drawing him out of his thoughts.

"That we can't dismiss her as a suspect. Brainard either as he could have hired someone. Money motivates many a crime."

"As does family honor."

"Yes." Hanlan stood. "What do you think of an early lunch since we have that appointment with Shaw just before 1 p.m.?"

Before Canin could answer, the Captain stood in the doorway. "That was interesting."

"She's clearly hiding something." Hanlan nodded.

"I agree. Go over the files Shaw has with a fine tooth comb. There's got to be a hint there somewhere at least."

"I intend to, Captain."

The Captain inclined her head, then left, heading back to her office.

"Well, Joey's?" Hanlan asked Canin. The burrito was long gone and he needed coffee again. No, he needed sleep but that seemed to be in short supply for him. So food would do.

"It's not even ten yet."

"Then Brunch," Hanlan said. "I'm hungry."

"Alright." Canin stood. "But you're buying."

"Deal."

CHAPTER 8

Brunch had consisted of Joey's breakfast special of eggs, bacon, and two pancakes with coffee. Thus fortified the two detectives returned to the station and filled out some paperwork. There was paperwork for everything one did. Canin updated the notes while Hanlan transcribed the interview.

Hanlan finished his bit of paperwork pretty quickly, then leaned back in his chair with a sigh. He had tried to get his partner to open up a bit while they were eating but Canin still wouldn't talk. Canin was holding something back. This Hanlan knew. Something troubling his gut told him. He had learned to listen to his gut a long time ago.

Which was telling him that there was something

unusual about this case. Something besides the obvious. Something that felt familiar. As if he had heard about it but had half forgotten it. So it nagged at him. Stirred his gut.

"So are we taking a couple of uniforms with us when we visit Shaw?"

Canin's voice interrupted Hanlan's thoughts and he looked at his partner. "No." Hanlan shook his head. "He'll cooperate once we show him the subpoena."

"I was thinking more of them being our mules if there's more than a few files."

"That's what you're for." Hanlan smiled at Canin.

Canin grimaced. "That's what I thought you'd say."

Hanlan gave a little laugh. Before he could say anything though his phone rang. He picked it up and said, "Hanlan." There was a long pause, then he said, "Thank you." before hanging up. "That was Dr. Brennon. The cause and manner were the same as the Graves'."

"So the case is officially ours now."

"Yep." He gave a little grin at Canin's irritated look.

Canin's cell phone rang and he pulled it out, answering with "Canin." He listened for a moment, then spoke again. "I see. Thank you for getting back to me. Have a nice day." He slipped the cell back in his inner jacket pocket before looking at Hanlan. "That was the manager of Lupo's apartment building. I had left that message earlier when we went to Joey's." He paused for Hanlan to nod acknowledgment. "Well it seems their camera for the front door has been off-line for the last twenty-four hours. So no footage for yesterday."

"Meaning Lupo doesn't have corroboration for her alibi."

"Nope." He empathized the p a bit.

Hanlan grinned at Canin for a minute then turned serious again. "The bodies will be released today."

"So the funeral."

"We'll ask Shaw." Hanlan glanced at the clock. "We should go."

Both detectives stood and Hanlan patted his jacket pocket before they headed for the double doors. They took the back elevator down, then hurried out the back and down the stairs. Hanlan slid into the driver's seat while Canin got in the passenger side.

The ride only took five minutes since the building was close to the station and Hanlan had already been here once. They made it to the sixth floor ten minutes ahead of their scheduled appointment time.

"I'm Detective Hanlan and this is my partner Detective Canin. We have an appointment with Mr. Stephan Shaw."

"Let me check." The receptionist flipped a page on her planner laying on her desk and ran a finger down, stopping half-way. "Here you are...His office is three doors down." She pointed to the hallway on the right. "Marie is waiting for you."

"After we finish with Mr. Shaw, we would like to talk to you about yesterday."

"Alright."

Hanlan gave her a nod, then he and Canin

headed toward the office she had pointed out. They stepped inside to a small office with a waiting area and a door on the one wall. It was decorated in earth tones with the secretary's desk and waiting area chairs being wood. The office was cozy and warm, not opulent like Shaw senior's had been.

"Detectives, I'm Marie Young, Mr. Shaw's secretary." The woman was middle-aged but had short styled black hair and a modest pantsuit on. She screamed reliable. "He's on the phone right now. Can I get you some coffee while you wait?"

"No, thank you." Hanlan shook his head. "But you can answer some questions if you don't mind about yesterday."

"Okay."

"When did you leave yesterday?"

"A little after five. I had just delivered Mr. Shaw a letter I had finished typing for him and left a few minutes later."

"You didn't see or hear anyone in the lobby or the main lobby downstairs?"

"No." She shook her head. "Of course I really wasn't paying any attention."

Hanlan nodded acknowledgment.

A buzzer went off on her desk and Marie touched a button. "The detectives are here."

"Send them in."

Marie gestured toward the closed door on the one wall and the two detectives headed there.

Stephan Shaw's office looked like a college professor's study. Worldly knick knacks and full bookshelves covered every inch of space except for the area around the wood desk and the wing back chairs set in front of it.

Hanlan liked it. He and Canin moved to the desk and shook Shaw's hand. When Shaw sat and gestured to the chairs, he and Canin sat themselves, leaning forward a bit.

"Before we get into the Graves', have you learned anything about my father's death?"

"Nothing probative," Hanlan told him.

Shaw nodded, then ask, "I suppose you have a subpoena?"

"Yes." Hanlan reached into his pocket and pulled out the envelope. He laid it on the edge of Shaw's desk.

Shaw pulled out a file from his desk and laid it in front of him. "I had planned to tell you about this during this meeting when Marie told me you set up this appointment. Mr. Graves had been getting these notes for the last six months. All unsigned. Anthony threw the first few away, but I had him give the others to me."

"What did they say?"

Pulling out a zip-lock bag, he held it up. In the baggie was scraps of paper. Shaw tossed it to Hanlan who caught it and looked at the bag.

"What is this 'it' that they refer to?"

"Anthony didn't know. At least that's what he told me." Shaw picked up the envelope from the edge of his desk and opened it, pulling out the subpoena. He glanced over it, then scooted the file toward them. "There's something else I figure you should know. There's a son, well, Claire's son and Anthony's stepson. What's pertinent is that when he was sixteen he tried to kill his stepfather."

"What?" Harlan looked at him sharply.

"Tried to beat him to death with a baseball bat." Shaw nodded. "He was locked away a couple of years for it. When he came out he threatened to kill them both. He's spent at least the last ten years in and out of Jail."

"His name?"

"Derick Reed."

"You know where he's at now?"

Shaw shook his head.

"We'll find him." Hanlan stood. "By the way, when's the funeral?"

"Tomorrow at 3 pm. Why?"

"We need to talk to his friends."

"He didn't keep in touch with his colleagues from the University. When he retired he cut those ties."

"Do you know why?"

"He called them back-stabbing savages. There is a protege he talked about a lot. He may be at the funeral. But he was on a sabbatical."

"This protege have a name?"

"Sam Ballerd, I think."

Canin had stood as well and had moved to the door as the other two had talked.

Shaw stood and shook Hanlan's hand again. "Please keep me informed. In both investigations."

"As much as I can." Hanlan hedged. "The funeral will be held at Ballday's?"

"Yes. He wanted a grand send-off."

Hanlan grabbed the file off the desk and headed toward the door. "See you at the funeral then, Mr. Shaw."

"Good day, Detectives."

Both detectives exited his office, then nodded to his secretary as they headed for the lobby. Once there they stopped at the reception desk.

The receptionist was a tiny thing but the glint in her pale eyes told of a steely spine. She was dressed in a silk ensemble that probably cost more than Hanlan made in a month but she radiated compassion and approachability.

"Ms. Nelson, when did you leave yesterday?" Hanlan asked her.

"Just after Marie. I usually stay until five-thirty but Mr. Shaw. Shaw Senior, that is, told me to go home. He seemed anxious to get rid of me."

"Oh?"

"Yeah. He hovered while I got my stuff together, then he escorted me to the door. I asked him if anything was wrong but he just shook his head and told me to have a good night. Perhaps if I had stayed..."

"We might have had two bodies. Don't play the 'what if' game."

Nelson nodded.

"Did you see anyone in the lobby downstairs?"

"A woman got on the elevator as I got off. But I wasn't paying attention so I didn't get a good look at her."

"Was she wearing a blue silk blouse and black pants and jacket?"

Ms. Nelson tilted her head and closed her eyes for a second before nodding. "Yes. I remember wondering where she got them."

"Thank you, Ms. Nelson."

"Brigitte, can you..." Marie broke off and stopped as she saw the two detectives at the receptionist's desk. "Excuse me, Detectives, I didn't know you were still here."

"That's all right, Ms. Young. We're done." Hanlan turned his attention back to the receptionist. "Thanks again, Ms. Nelson."

The receptionist nodded, then looked at Marie. "Did you need something, Marie?"

Both detectives left the firm and headed for the elevator. They rode down in silence.

As they made to pass the security desk, the guard stood and waved to grab their attention. "Detectives."

"Mr. Hastings," Hanlan said as he and Canin stopped. "What can we do for you?"

"I just wanted to tell you about an incident that happened day before yesterday. Mr. Shaw Senior had just come in when this man accosted him. I didn't hear what was said, but the man went away angry. Mr. Shaw just brushed it off when I said something and went upstairs. I got Mr. Harvey to make you a copy of the incident." He handed Hanlan a VHS tape. "I didn't recognize the man."

"Thanks." Hanlan took the tape.

Hastings nodded and sat back down as the detectives continued to head for the front doors.

"Who do you think it is? Brainard?" Canin asked.

"Could be the son."

They paused just outside the front doors, holding the one open for a woman to enter before heading toward their car.

Once at the car, Hanlan slid in the driver's side and set the file and the tape on the storage arm between the front seats. He waited until Canin was settled in the passenger seat before he spoke. "I think Mr. Shaw was holding something back. Something about Graves' colleagues."

"You caught that too."

"Yes. I want you to do a little digging on the University while I look into the son."

"Alright."

Hanlan started the vehicle and headed toward the station. They had a lot of work ahead of them.

CHAPTER 9

The detectives headed straight to the conference room once they got to the station and upstairs. Canin sat on the table again as Hanlan slipped in the tape.

Neither of them recognized the man arguing with Robert Shaw. He was shorter than Shaw with a goatee and scraggly dark hair and wearing a white tee with torn jeans. Not the kind of person who would normally be a client of a successful firm like Shaw Consulting. Yet Shaw seem to know him.

Hanlan retrieved the tape and handed it to Canin. "Would you mind taking it to the Lab?"

Canin slid off the table and disappeared out the door.

Before Hanlan could head out the door himself,

the Captain appeared. "I had Sgt. Dan call me when you returned. Give me an update."

He gave her a brief rundown of what happened, then handed her the zip-lock from his jacket's outer pocket. "I'm going to look through them before I hand it in to the Lab."

She nodded in agreement as she glanced at the notes, then handed the baggie back to him. "Any insights you want to tell me?"

"You know I don't work like that."

"No, you keep everything close to your vest." The Captain paused. "How is the partnership going?" she asked suddenly.

"He doesn't talk much," he told her.

"Is that good or bad?"

"I'll let you know."

"I'm sure you will." She nodded. "I'll let you get back to work."

They both exited the conference room and headed into the bullpen. However she continued on to her office while Hanlan stopped at his desk.

The file went on his desk as he sat down and he leaned into his computer. He typed in the son's name and got immediate results.

Canin slid into his chair and got on his own computer.

"Derick Reed just went up the suspect list."

"Oh?" Canin looked over at Hanlan.

"Not only is he the man we saw arguing with Shaw, but he got arrested last night at a dog fight."

"What?"

"The One-Six busted a dog fighting ring with connections to a drug gang last night. Abandoned building on Blinker. According to the report, Reed was one of the organizers of the fight."

"Can we question him?"

"I'll get the Captain to put in the request."

Canin nodded, then returned his attention to his own computer. "There's not much here. Though there was some kind of scandal at the University five years ago."

"Oh?" Hanlan straightened and looked at Canin. "That's when Graves retired."

"Seems there's some sort of gag order."

Hanlan grabbed the file they had gotten from Shaw and opened it. He flipped through the papers, then stopped as he found what he was looking for. "Here we go. The gag order was filed by Shaw. A fellow professor accused Graves of stealing her work. She even assaulted him. It seems his retirement was part of a settlement."

"Does it say what her 'work' was?"

"No." Hanlan shook his head. He closed the file and shoved it back on his desk before standing. "I'm going to talk to the Captain."

Canin gave him a little wave of acknowledgment but didn't raise his eyes from his computer screen.

A moment later Hanlan was standing in the Captain's office doorway. She looked up at him when he cleared his throat.

"Something new, Detective?"

"Yes." He nodded. "We need to request a prisoner be brought here from the One-Six for questioning."

She raised an eyebrow.

He explained who Derick Reed was and what he

had been arrested for. "He had means but we need to see if he had opportunity."

"I'll put in the request but you know it will probably be tomorrow morning before they process it."

"As long as we can make the funeral."

"Alright." She gave a nod, then looked at him again. "Anything else, Detective?"

Hanlan explained about the gag order and the scandal. "I'm not sure how to go about getting more information without ruffling feathers."

"Hmm. Let me do a little investigating of my own before you do any more digging in that area."

"Okay." He paused. "Although we might run into her at the funeral."

"I'll get back to you before the funeral."

"Alright." He turned to leave, then looked back at her. "This is getting more complicated instead of less."

"Then go make it less so."

Hanlan grunted, then headed back to his desk. He slid into his chair and looked at Canin. "Did you find out anything else?"

"Nothing probative," Canin told him. "But I did find something interesting." He paused as he looked over at Hanlan. "The University bought the Manor for Graves. I called them while you were with the Captain to ensure I had it right. He had them make the Manor an enticement to keep him at their college."

"Did they know why?"

"No." Canin shook his head. "But when a famous anthropologist makes a simple request to keep lending his personage to your college I guess you don't ask questions."

"Famous? I've never heard of him."

"You're not reading the right books and magazines then. Twenty years ago he was at the top of his field. Even now in certain circles his name is brandied about. But he was on his way down. He hadn't published in five years and in anthropology that's bad. Publish or Perish."

"What was his last publication about?"

Canin typed on his computer, then said, "It was an article called 'Those Hidden Among Us'. He proposed that there are beings of a different race hidden among humans. That they were the fact behind some myths and legends."

Hanlan had a thoughtful look on his face. Something his Grandmother had said to him as a child tugged at him.

"What are you thinking?" Canin asked softly.

Shaking his head, Hanlan pushed the nagging tug of memory to the back of his mind and pulled his attention back to the present. "Nothing. Just woolgathering. He didn't publish anything else after that?"

"If he did I can't find it." He paused. "What was her name?"

"Jennifer Lowell. She was a Teaching Assistant five years ago so she should be a professor by now."

"She is. Lots of articles on digs she went on in the last five years. Most about how language influenced the culture. Seems to have made a name for herself among certain circles with these articles.

Finally settled as a professor six months ago at the University."

"Six months." Hanlan pulled out the zip-lock with the notes. "Shaw said Graves was getting these notes for the last six months." He opened the baggie and lifted one of the hand-written notes out of it. "The writing could be feminine."

"The Lab will be able to tell."

Hanlan dumped the notes on his desk and read through them quickly. They were all brief and accused Graves of finding and keeping something to himself. Some were vaguely threatening while others were just accusatory. And none named what that something was. He put the notes back in the baggie, then tossed the baggie to Canin.

"Find anything?"

"Nothing probative. Will you take that down to the Lab?"

"Am I to be your Go-for?"

He flashed a brief smile at Canin. "Yep."

Canin rolled his eyes, then stood and headed off for the Lab.

Glancing at the clock, Hanlan leaned back in his chair. He was ready to call it a night and get something to take home. There was that last file, the Cummings disappearance, to get through. Maybe something from it would trigger something and he'd catch something. There was a lot of somethings in that thought.

Howell appeared at his desk with two large envelopes which he tossed on Hanlan's desk. "Pictures of the Shaw crime scene. They delivered them to us. I was in court and Deneque was following a lead so we didn't notice them until now."

"Thanks." Hanlan opened one of the envelopes and pulled out the pictures.

"Making any progress?"

"Four suspects instead of one." Hanlan flipped through the photos, then returned them to their envelope before opening the other one. He pulled out those pictures and flipped through them.

Howell chuckled.

Canin returned and nodded to Howell as he slid into his seat.

Hanlan put the photos back in their envelope, then handed both to Canin before looking at Howell. "Thanks again, Howell. I'll tell you how it ends up."

Howell nodded and headed back to his own desk.

"I'm calling it a day." Hanlan stood and stretched. "I'm going to grab something to eat and read the Cummings file. I'll bring it in tomorrow for you."

"Alright." Canin opened one of the envelopes. "I'll just look through these, then go. See you in the morning."

Hanlan nodded and headed out of the bullpen. He'd pick something up at Chickie's again. A drink would be good as well as he read that file.

Perhaps he might even get some real sleep tonight.

CHAPTER 10

Morning had found him on his couch. He had fallen asleep reading the file, but it hadn't been a peaceful sleep. Blood-covered wolves had attacked him again in his dreams.

He had microwaved some pancakes and had eaten them as he'd finished reading the file. Coffee had gone into a travel mug and he had been out the door within an hour of waking with the file in hand. The drive to the station had been done in record time as he had hit almost no traffic. A rare happening.

Canin was at his desk when Hanlan made it to the bullpen. Hanlan dropped the file on Canin's desk then slid into his own chair. "The Cummings file. An interesting read."

"Oh?" Canin grabbed the file and flipped through it. "How so?"

"No signs of a struggle. No blood. Everything in its place. The investigating officers even stated that it looked like they had just stepped out."

"But they'd been missing for a while by that time, hadn't they?"

"Yep." Hanlan flashed him a grin at Canin's irritated look. He didn't think that would ever get old, irritating Canin with one word. "Neighbors reported that they hadn't seen them in over a week. One of them had finally called us or the Cummings would never have been reported missing."

"No John or Jane Does?"

"Not then or since that fit them. The M.E.'s office has standing orders to check every John or Jane Doe to see if they match the Cummings."

Canin closed the file and set it on his desk on top of the Raven Manor murder files. "That is interesting."

"Reed will be here in an hour," the Captain said as she appeared beside Hanlan's desk. "A Vice detective from the One-Six will be sitting in on the interrogation."

"We the screwer or the screwee?"

The Captain shrugged.

"Which room?"

"Two. I'll be in Observation."

Hanlan nodded to her and she headed back to her office as he turned to Canin. "The detective will probably be Anderson. If it is I just want to warn you. We have some history between us."

"Okay," Canin said, drawing out the word a bit.

Anderson, Hanlan knew, would be more than willing to tell Canin all about it without Canin even asking as Anderson knew Hanlan wouldn't talk about it. Hanlan wasn't that kind of person. But Anderson wouldn't miss an opportunity for a dig.

Dr. Brennon appeared at Hanlan's desk with a file in her arms.

"You know you didn't have to bring the report yourself," Hanlan said, looking at her.

"I wanted to make sure it got here."

"What do you mean?" Hanlan raised an eyebrow.

"My copies of the official reports on the Graves are missing."

"What?"

"I came in this morning early to check something and found them missing. The individual test results are still there, thank god, so I can redo the reports. But the official reports are gone."

"Someone didn't just misplace them?" Canin asked.

Dr. Brennon just stared at him for a minute, then said simply, "No."

"Is CSU at the Morgue?" Hanlan asked her.

"Yes, and a Detective Nettle."

"Okay. I'll give him a call later."

"I thought you should know." Dr. Brennon laid the report on Hanlan's desk. "I didn't know if they would say anything to you about it."

"Depends upon the detective and the Captain."

Dr. Brennon gave a nod, then headed off toward the front doors.

"There seems to be something going on besides a simple murder," Canin said.

"Simple?" Hanlan pulled the autopsy report closer. "This was never simply about murder." He flipped through the report. "Raven Manor has a secret that people are willing to kill for."

Canin opened his mouth but closed it as movement nearby drew his attention. "They're bringing in Reed," he told Hanlan a minute later.

Hanlan closed the autopsy report and shoved it away before standing. He led the way back to the interview rooms and stopped outside of number two. "Like the old saying, 'get your game face on'."

Both detectives took a breath and blanked their faces, then Hanlan opened the door.

Inside was the dark-haired man from the video and an older blond man. Both were seated at the table facing the mirrored wall. Reed was dressed in an orange jumpsuit while the other man was wearing a nice dark suit.

"Detective Anderson, this is my partner Detective Canin," Hanlan said as he and Canin moved to the other chairs. They sat down as the other detective gave Canin a nod. "Have you informed Mr. Reed why he was being brought here?"

"No." Anderson shook his head. "Figured you'd want to do that."

"Mr. Reed, I'm Detective Hanlan. I have some questions for you regarding the death of your mother and stepfather."

Reed just stared at Hanlan.

"You did inform him of their deaths, didn't you, Detective Anderson?"

"Well, I'm sure someone did."

"They're really dead?" Reed asked Hanlan, ignoring Anderson.

"Yes." Hanlan paused, then spoke again. "Where were you three days ago between 5 and 6:30 pm.?"

Reed glared at him but didn't speak.

"How about two days ago between those same times?"

A knock came, then the door opened to reveal an officer with Brainard standing there. The officer nodded to Hanlan, then left.

"This interview is over," Brainard said as he stepped inside. "I need a few minutes with my client."

"Client?" Both Hanlan and Anderson asked together.

"Yes." Brainard gave a tight smile. "Now if you would please allow me time with my client?"

All three detectives left the interview room and gathered in Observation with the Captain. The sound was off and the blind was pulled down so they couldn't see into the interview room.

"How did he get a private lawyer?" Anderson asked grumpily.

"Ms. Lupo." Hanlan said. "She's making a play for the Manor through helping Reed."

"Is he the beneficiary of Graves' Will?" the captain asked.

"Who's Ms. Lupo?" Anderson asked at the same time.

Canin drew Anderson away to give him a run

down of their case while Hanlan answered the captain.

"The Will wasn't in the file Shaw gave us. But I doubt Reed is the beneficiary."

"Oh?"

"Reed tried to kill his stepfather when he was younger."

"Then what does Ms. Lupo gain by helping him?"

"If there's no Will or it's invalidated in some way, he would be the beneficiary. Also if we're busy with him we won't be investigating her."

"Covering her bases." The captain gave a nod. "A risk but the reward would be worth it to her."

A knock on the glass sent the three detectives back to the interview room. Brainard was sitting beside Reed who was not looking happy. Anderson leaned against the wall by the door while Hanlan and Canin moved to the table.

"My client has nothing to say to you, Detectives, and demands to be returned to the Sixteenth Precinct."

"You don't want to make a statement?" Hanlan asked Reed.

"As I said he has nothing to say to you," Brainard said before Reed could do more than open his mouth. The lawyer looked over his shoulder at Anderson. "You need to return him to your precinct."

Anderson straightened and moved to Reed. He helped Reed to stand and turned him towards the door. "Sorry, Hanlan."

"I'll meet you at your precinct, Detective

Anderson." Brainard stood as Anderson led Reed from the room. "If you want to talk to my client again call me and we'll consider it," the lawyer told Hanlan before leaving the room himself.

"Detectives." The Captain appeared in the doorway. "I'm going to have them send over his file, both hard copy and through email."

"Better do it fast. I have a feeling Brainard will try to stall any investigation or information sharing he can."

The Captain nodded, then disappeared back to her office.

"How about we do some paperwork, then have an early lunch. Reed's file should be here by the time we get back. We can dive into it before we leave for the funeral."

"Sounds good to me," Canin said as he followed Hanlan out the door.

CHAPTER 11

After lunch the physical file on Reed had indeed been on Hanlan's desk but there hadn't been much in it as the dog fighting case had just started. The basics were there like his job at the dog shelter and his current address which was in the One-Six's area as well as a list of known associates. Hanlan and Canin looked the associates up but didn't find much there either. Most were in jail or dead. A few were in the drug gang One-Six was investigating but that was One-Six's territory and Hanlan wasn't going to step on Anderson's toes.

At least not yet.

Hanlan brought the Captain up-to-date, then headed back to his desk. He and Canin had had a quiet lunch, neither talking much as they both were sunk into their own thoughts. Usually he like to get his partners' thoughts on cases to help solidify his own but he was still wary of Canin. Canin was hiding something. Something serious. He trusted Canin enough to work with him but not enough to put himself out there.

"I updated the notes." Canin turned away from his computer. "What can I expect from this funeral? I never attended one at Ballday's. I heard they're different than normal funerals."

"They are." Hanlan leaned back in his chair. "It is more like an Irish Wake combined with a New Orleans funeral. The music is Jazz, heavy on the sax, and there is food and drink, mostly alcohol. Elegies about the deceased are given. It's more a party than a funeral."

"And people pay for this?"

"It's all the vogue right now for the Nouveau Riche. If you got money you need to go out in style."

"Style?"

"That's the way it's sold." Hanlan shrugged with his hands up.

Canin grunted.

Glancing at the clock, Hanlan scooted his chair back and stood. "I want to get there before the others and talk to Shaw so we better leave now."

Nodding, Canin stood as well. "Okay."

Both detectives headed out of the bullpen toward the back elevator. They rode down in silence. Sgt. Dan gave them a wave as they went past to the doors and they gave him a nod. Hanlan held the door open for an inbound detective, then followed

Canin down the stairs. At the car Hanlan slid into the driver's seat as Canin got in the passenger side.

"Are you ever going to let me drive?"

"This vehicle is signed out to me. So no." Hanlan started the car and backed out. He straightened it and drove around the building into traffic.

Ballday was at the edge of their station's main downtown area. The stone building had once been a library but Robert Ballday had bought it and renovated it into a unique funeral home years ago. His son and daughter ran it now and had been the ones that had come up with their special funeral package. They did a normal funeral package as well but most that came to Ballday's did the deluxe. It was what they were best known for.

Hanlan pulled into the mostly empty parking lot and parked near as he could get to the building but slightly to the side. He didn't want to get parked in by anyone.

Both detectives got out and headed up the small but wide bit of stairs to the decorative front doors. Hanlan held the door for Canin, then followed him inside.

The carpeted lobby had a hallway leading back and a small office to the left with a door to the right. A young woman dressed in a dark dress came out of the office.

"Hello, Gentlemen. I'm Mary Calendar. How may I help you?"

"I'm Detective Hanlan and this is my partner Detective Canin. We're here for the Graves Affair. We were hoping to catch Mr. Shaw before the activities began."

"Ah, yes. Mr. Shaw said you'd be stopping by." She pointed to the other door. "He's in the Ballroom."

"Thank you," Hanlan told her before both detectives went to the door. He opened the door, then followed Canin through the door before closing it behind himself.

Tables and chairs were spaced throughout the very large room. In the center were two closed coffins with a decorated table between them. Buffet tables were set along the right wall and servers were moving about them. Shaw was standing by the decorated table and that was where the detectives headed.

"Detectives," Shaw greeted as they came up to him. "You're a bit early."

"I wanted to ask you why a copy of the Will wasn't in that file you gave us." Hanlan got straight to the point. He didn't know how long they would have the room to themselves. Well, besides the staff.

Shaw lifted a sealed envelope from the decorated table and waved it at Hanlan. "Because it's right here, Detective. I'm to unseal it and read it an hour after this 'shindig' starts."

"And you have no idea what it says?"

"Father might have." Shaw shook his head. "But I don't."

"I want you to introduce me to the professor that accused Graves, if she shows up. We need to ask her some questions."

"That I can do. But you understand I can't talk

about the case except about what is the file? And neither can she. The gag order pertains to me as well as her. Graves wanted it that way."

"I just need her to establish her whereabouts this last week, not anything about the case."

"Alright." Shaw slipped the envelope back underneath the open book on the table. "Will you be wanting to look at the Guest Book afterwards?"

"We'll have an officer pick it up tomorrow from your office."

Shaw nodded, then looked over toward the main door. "They're starting to arrive."

"Canin, why don't you mingle? I'll stay with Shaw."

His partner nodded, then headed toward the six people hovering at the door. They were all dressed in black suits and dresses. The three men looked around for a moment, then headed for the buffet table where the alcohol was while the women stayed by the door, talking. Canin changed course and followed the men toward the alcohol table.

"They're some of Graves' fellow professors and the women are their wives. Anthony and Claire socialized with them at University functions but they were not friends. At least not to Graves," Shaw told Hanlan. "He took being their boss seriously and they were major suck-ups."

"So you don't think they'd have the stones to kill Graves?" Hanlan kept an eye on both the door and the alcohol table.

"Or the constitution."

Hanlan glanced at him.

"I saw their bodies and—my father's." Shaw

reminded him. "Too gory. Blood or no blood."

A tall dark-haired young woman in a dark skirt and white blouse entered the room. She ignored the wives as she moved away from the door, but she didn't head toward the men either. As she glanced around Hanlan noticed her hair was in a tight bun at the back of her head and he suspected she had come straight from work. Her head turned toward Shaw and Hanlan and she immediately headed their way.

"Professor Jennifer Lowell, this is Detective Hanlan," Shaw said as soon as the woman reached them. "He would like to speak to you."

Lowell's cognac eyes settled on the detective as she seemed to sniff the air. She frowned at him. "About what?"

"Your whereabouts three days ago between 5 and 6:30 pm. as well as two days ago between the same time."

"That is none of your business." Her voice was cold.

"Afraid it is, Ms. Lowell. We can either discuss it here civilly or at the station."

Canin appeared at Hanlan's side, his cognac eyes on Lowell.

"I'll come in to your station tomorrow morning around nine." She took two steps back and whirled, heading for the alcohol table.

"Did you find out anything?" Hanlan asked Canin.

"Nothing probative."

Hanlan raised an eyebrow.

"They all think Graves was having an affair with Lowell and when he wouldn't leave his wife for her she caused the dust up."

Shaw snorted.

"Yeah, I got the feeling they'd get frostbite if anyone touched her," Hanlan said.

"A burn more like," Shaw told him. "Her demeanor may be cold but her temper can be fiery. She nearly lost control several times during the case but her lawyer kept her on a tight leash. I'd advise you to be careful, Detective."

"Thanks for the information, Mr. Shaw." Hanlan turned his attention back to Canin. "Anything else from the professors?"

"Just that they don't like the new Chair."

"What about Ms. Lowell?"

"They're envious of her, I think. But they seem to like her well enough, though they blame her for the dust up and the new Chair."

Hanlan frowned thoughtfully. He had the same gut feeling about Lowell as he did about Lupo. There was something about both of them that was visceral. Something that made him instinctively dislike them. Something inherently evil.

Three older people entered the room and paused just inside the door. The woman was dressed in an older dark dress while the two men wore brown corduroy suits. As soon as the woman caught sight of Shaw, the group headed toward him.

"Mrs. Carson, glad you could make it," Shaw said as the three stopped in front of him. "I was afraid you'd be too busy to attend."

"After everything Anthony did for the Trust how could I not." She paused as she gestured to the men with her. "This is Dr. Keller and Dr. Stevenson, members of the Trust's board."

"Gentlemen." Shaw gave them a nod. "These are Detectives Hanlan and Canin. They are looking into Anthony and Claire's deaths."

"Detectives," Carson said as the two men gave the detectives nods.

Hanlan and Canin returned the nods and Hanlan said, "Nice to meet you, Mrs. Carson. I've heard a lot about the Trust's good work."

Mrs. Carson smiled at Hanlan but before she could say anything Shaw cleared his throat and rang a little bell from the table. He retrieved the sealed envelope as everyone gathered in front of him. "Mr. Graves wanted his Will read once everyone was gathered..." He broke off as he looked past the group in front of him.

Wanting to see what caused him to stop, Hanlan followed his gaze.

Reed and Brainard stood just inside the door.

CHAPTER 12

"You weren't going to start without me, were you, Mr. Shaw?" Reed smirked as he and Brainard moved further into the room.

"Remove yourself from the premises, Mr. Reed. You were not invited." Shaw's voice was calm though fury flared in his eyes.

"As her nearest relative, I have a right to be here."

Shaw pulled out an envelope from his jacket pocket. "Not according to this restraining order."

Reed snatched the envelope from Shaw's hand and tore it in half, letting it fall to the floor. "What restraining order? Besides they are dead."

"Mr. Brainard, if you do not leave with your

client right now, I will arrest him." Hanlan looked at Brainard. "And you."

Brainard had a speculative look in his eyes.

"Canin..."

His partner stepped forward, reaching for the cuff's at his back.

"Mr. Reed," Canin began. "You have the..."

"Alright," Brainard interrupted as he half turned away. "Come along, Mr. Reed."

Reed didn't move.

"Mr. Reed." There was a warning tone in Brainard's voice.

"This isn't the end of this." Reed whirled and both he and Brainard headed away.

"Thank you, Detectives," Shaw said.

Canin returned his cuffs where they belonged, then moved back to Hanlan's side.

Shaw waited until Brainard and Reed were out the door before he turned his attention back to the group. "I am sorry about that." He tore open the large envelope and pulled out the Will. His eyes ran over it and he frowned.

"Everything okay, Mr. Shaw?" Hanlan asked.

"Yes. Yes." He cleared his throat and began to read the Will out loud. "I, Anthony Graves, being of sound mind and body, do bequeath the following. My moneys and such tangibles go to my wife if she survives me. If not it is to be put in a Trust for the Alsena Historical Society and Trust, the interest distributed and run by Shaw Consulting annually for the upkeep of Raven Manor. Raven Manor itself is to be given to the Alsena Historical Society and Trust with the stipulation that if my wife is still alive, she is to be allowed to live there until her death. Also they are not allowed to sell it or my moneys and such will be put in a Trust run by Shaw Consulting to maintain the Manor for as long as it lasts. It is signed by Mr. Graves. Below his signature is a note from Mrs. Graves that says her will is as his."

"That bastard!" Lowell virtually growled.

"Control yourself, Ms. Lowell," Canin said in an authoritative voice as he stepped forward. "This is not the time or place."

She glared at him, then whirled and glided out of the room.

Hanlan shot Canin a glance but didn't comment.

"Oh, my," Mrs. Carson gasped.

The two men with her looked just as stunned.

"We can get together in a couple of days and settle things," Shaw told her. He then gestured. "Until then. Everyone enjoy this last 'shindig' of Anthony's."

The professors headed straight back to the alcohol, their wives whispering harshly. Shaw stepped aside with the Trust group to set up a time for a meeting Hanlan guessed.

"We staying for the rest of it?" Canin asked.

"No. We accomplished what we needed for right now." Hanlan waved to Shaw who gave him a nod before turning back to the Trust group.

Both detectives left the ballroom and waved to Ms. Calendar as they headed for the front doors.

It was barely light outside. Storm clouds had moved in and the wind was gusting. Rain was in the air.

"I'll drop you off at the station." Hanlan got in the driver's side as Canin slid into the passenger seat. "I'm going to call it a day."

"Sounds good to me too."

Hanlan drove carefully as the rain started to come down when they left Ballday's. They rode in silence, their minds absorbing what they had just learned. Soon they were at the station and Hanlan pulled up close to the stairs. "I'll see you in the morning, Canin."

Canin nodded, then jumped out of the car and ran up the stairs.

As soon as he was sure his partner was inside, Hanlan pulled a way and headed home. He went through a drive-thru on the way as he was hungry and still made good time back to his apartment, even through the rain. As he parked in his slot, the rain seemed to slacken and he hurried to get out. He was half way to his door when something stopped him.

The hairs on the back of his neck were raised. He heard a growl from behind him and he slowly turned around.

A huge gray wolf was next to his car, slowing stalking forward. It's cognac eyes were more red than brown and almost glowed. Another low growl came from it as it hunched its hind legs. It was getting ready to spring yet Hanlan was frozen in place.

From his right came a black blur. It collided with the gray wolf, knocking the gray to the ground. The gray rolled away, then leaped to its feet to confront the giant black wolf. They stood there motionless for a moment, glaring at each other, then the gray disappeared in the gloom. The black wolf glanced at Hanlan with soft cognac eyes before it too vanished into the mists, leaving Hanlan to stare into the wet darkness.

Thunder rumbled across the sky, breaking him out of his shock. He slowly turned and headed toward his door. Impressions from his dreams mixed with images of what had just happened, making him clumsy with the key as he struggled to open his door. He finally entered and closed the door behind him, locking it automatically. The food went on the table and he nearly fell into his chair as emotion overwhelmed him.

His elbows went on the table and he buried his head in his hands. He had looked into the gray's eyes and seen his death. Death like the Graves', like Shaw's. That gray wolf was the killer, he was sure of that.

Once he calmed enough, he stood and put the food in the refrigerator. He didn't think he'd be able to eat. Now that he was calmer, his mind went over the event again, seeking details, to rationalize. It was both a blessing and a curse to have an inquiring mind like his. He got himself some whiskey, then went into the living room and slumped on the couch.

Rewind and start at the beginning.

Does it begin with the Graves or the murders that happened before? He didn't come into it until the Graves so he would start there. The big three: means, motive, and opportunity.

Suspect number one: The son Derick Reed. He

has access to vicious animals through the dog fighting ring and drug gang. No alibi established. The motive is shaky as he would know that Graves wouldn't leave him anything. Unless he just wanted to finish what he started when he was sixteen.

Suspect number two: Julia Lupo. With her money she could get anything she wanted except it seems Raven Manor so a vicious animal wouldn't be hard. No alibi since the cameras weren't working. The motive is definitely control of Raven Manor.

Suspect number three: Jennifer Lowell. The motive is also control of Raven Manor. However, the other two, means and opportunity, are on hold until the interview tomorrow.

Suspect number four: the lawyer Brainard. Suspected motive is money. If he gets Raven Manor for Ms. Lupo, he would get a large chunk of change. With his suspected connections it would be easy to get a vicious animal and have someone carry out the murders. It would have to be murder for hire as he was in his office at suspected time of death. But for a big payout, he might have done just that.

Now you add in Robert Shaw's murder.

Suspect number one would be Julia Lupo. Someone resembling her entered the building and got on the elevator. She doesn't have an established alibi.

But the Graves' son Reed was seen arguing with Shaw the day before. So he is a contender as well as Ms. Lowell since she could have been the woman seen. Unlikely but possible.

He needed to establish Brainard's whereabouts for Shaw's murder.

The attempted attack on him.

Hanlan took a sip of the whiskey and enjoyed the burn as he swallowed. Thus fortified he thought about the attempt.

There had been a cold intelligence in those glowing eyes. It knew what it was doing. Had the other wolf not challenged it, it would have killed him as it had the Graves and Shaw. The question was who had set it upon him?

Wolves. There was something about wolves that kept nagging at him. Then it hit him.

His great grandmother. She had told him stories about wolves when he was little before she had died. It tugged at his mind but he just couldn't recall any of them. When she had died he had become angry, grief-stricken, and had shoved all memory of her away. Now he barely remembered her or her pageant for stories. But she had been on his mind since he had started this case.

Del Mulanti Ruv

That is what she called the wolves in her tales. He still couldn't recall the stories themselves, but he remembered that name. Even now it caused a shiver of both excitement and fear like it had when he was little, even though he didn't remember why.

He took another sip of whiskey and enjoyed the burn again as he thought of the two wolves. The gray had elicited a visceral fear and hatred but the black had seem to radiate warmth. While he thought he knew why the gray had come, he wondered about the black. Why *had* he stopped the gray? Was someone protecting him?

Hanlan tossed back the rest of the whiskey and set the glass on the coffee table. He was tired but he had a feeling his dreams would be filled with gray wolves. Blood-covered gray wolves like the last couple of nights. More vivid since he had seen one in the flesh, so to speak. The alcohol would help him get to sleep, but he knew with the dreams it would be a restless night again.

He stretched out on the couch and closed his eyes. No use to try and sleep in his bed. The alcohol and his tiredness soon sent him into Morpheus' arms where the wolves dwelled.

CHAPTER 13

Morning dawned bright and clear. The storm had past.

A black wolf had chased away the other dream wolves and Hanlan had actually gotten some sleep. Though the wolves had kept coming back to be chased away again.

He had his take-out from last night as breakfast with a lot of coffee. To show mercy to his partner he showered and shaved and put on a clean suit before he left for the station. The little traffic that he hit meant he got there in good time.

Canin was at his desk when Hanlan made it to the bullpen.

"It seems we riled someone up," Hanlan said as he slid into his chair.

"Oh?" Canin looked at him with a raised eyebrow

"Yep."

Canin gave him an irritated look and Hanlan smiled but didn't say anything else.

"Are you going to tell me what happened or what?" Canin asked, exasperated.

"The murderer sent his killer after me last night."

"What?!"

"I was visited by a killer wolf last night outside my apartment."

"It obviously didn't kill you."

"No. It was chased off by another wolf."

Canin looked at him, his cognac eyes studying him. "You don't seem upset."

"The attempted attack means we're getting close. One of our four suspects is getting nervous about our investigation."

"And the wolf getting away?"

Hanlan shrugged.

"Professor Lowell is supposed to be here at nine," Canin said, changing the subject. "Do you think she'll actually show?"

"If she's got nothing to hide. Or at least wants to make us think she has nothing to hide."

The Captain appeared at Hanlan's desk, a slim file in her hand. "I'm sorry that I wasn't able to get back to you before the funeral yesterday but it took some finagling to get this." She handed the file to Hanlan who took it and flipped through it.

"Is this what I think it is?"

"Yes," The Captain nodded. "A copy of the thesis and notes used as evidence against Graves."

"Can we use this in Court?" Hanlan looked up at her.

"Yes. As evidence toward motive anyway."

Hanlan nodded, then went back to looking the file over.

"I'll leave you to it then, Detectives." The captain headed back to her office.

"Well?" Canin asked impatient.

"She speculated that legends, specifically the werewolf and vampire legends, were based off a race of beings that lived along side humans."

"Graves' last article speculated something similar."

"Thus her suit, I'm sure." Hanlan frowned. Some of what she expounded upon resonated in his mind as if he had been told something like it yet he didn't remember hearing it. He shook his head and closed the file, setting it on his desk. "I've been thinking that we should delay releasing Raven Manor for at least a few more days."

"Why?"

"It seems to be in the middle of this mire. And I want to go back there again."

"Oh?"

"There is something unusual about that place. Everything that has happened there has made me curious."

"Curiosity killed the cat, you know."

"Then good thing I'm not a cat or I would have been dead a long time ago." Hanlan glanced at the clock. "Want to update the notes or should I?"

"I'll do it." Canin slid closer to his computer.

Hanlan's phone rang and he picked it up with a

"Hanlan." He listened for a few minutes, then said, "Thanks" before hanging up. "That was the Lab. Two foreign fingerprints. No match in AFIS. They found more wolf hair on the clothes. The foreign DNA around what was left of the throat couldn't be identified as they got inconclusive results so they're running it again."

"We'll have to print our suspects as well as get DNA."

"Brainard's should be on file. He was a public defender once upon a time."

"Still leaves the other three." Canin got to work on the computer.

"I'll see if I can get the Captain to do the warrants." Hanlan pushed his chair back and stood. "Be back in a minute."

Canin nodded but didn't turn his attention from the computer screen.

Hanlan headed to the Captain's office and stood in the doorway when he got there. "Captain?"

"Yes." She looked up from her desk.

"We're going to need warrants to gather fingerprints and DNA from our four suspects."

She raised an eyebrow.

"They'll be expedited if you do them."

"I see." She paused. "Alright, Detective. I'll have the One-Six do the collecting for Brainard and Lupo and send over Reed's."

"Thank you, Captain." He half turned, then looked back at her. "It's getting more and more complicated instead of less."

"I told you to make it less so, not more."

"I have a feeling there are layers we haven't got

to yet."

"Well, discover them and sort through this mess. Preferably before we have another body."

He gave her a two finger salute, then headed back to his desk. Glancing at the clock, he slid into his chair and looked at Canin. "Ten 'til."

Canin also glance at the clock, then went back to his computer screen. "You want to make that bet?"

"Be a sucker's bet either way."

His partner shrugged.

Hanlan watched the minutes, then seconds count down as Canin finished the notes. When Canin slid his chair back from the computer, Hanlan spoke. "Nine Oh One." Hanlan's phone didn't ring. He typed her name into his computer.

"Well?"

"We'll have to have the One-Eight pay her a visit. She lives near the University." Hanlan's phone rang and he answered with "Hanlan." A pause, then, "Mr. Shaw, what can I do for you?" Another pause. "We'll release the place in another four days." This pause was longer. "We want to ensure we have all the evidence." A short pause. "Thank you. Goodbye, Mr. Shaw." Hanlan hung up the phone.

"You still want to go there again?"

"I haven't changed my mind in the last hour or so no."

"I thought that might have been her with an excuse."

"So did I." Hanlan pushed his chair back and stood. "Guess I should see the Captain again."

"See me about what?" the Captain asked as she came up to Hanlan's desk.

Hanlan explained to her about Lowell's outburst and the missed appointment as he sat back down and leaned back in his chair. "You'll have to talk to the One-eight about collecting DNA and prints plus this," he told her at the end of the explanation.

"I'll talk to the One-Eight but it will probably be tomorrow afternoon or the next day before we hear back from them. The One-Six should be back to us tomorrow."

"I know." Hanlan shrugged. "See what I mean about complicated?"

"Do you have any theories?"

"Several."

She raised an eyebrow.

"I need more data before I share."

"That's what you said about the Osborne case and you arrested the killer before you shared."

Hanlan gave her a smile as he shrugged.

"I hope he's more forthcoming with you, Detective," she said to Canin.

Canin just gave her a bland face and a shrug.

She threw up her hands in exasperation, then whirled and headed for her office.

"Are you going to share with me?" Canin asked.

Hanlan stared at him for a minute, then stood. "Let's get some coffee."

CHAPTER 14

Almost an hour later, they were seated at a picnic bench in Alsena's Poet Park near Raven Manor's neighborhood. Hanlan had taken them through a drive-thru for coffee, then driven straight here. It was quiet and no one would be able to overhear their conversation.

"I know you are keeping something from me." Hanlan got straight to the point. "Something dangerous."

Canin raised an eyebrow.

"My brain tells me to be wary, yet I want to trust you. You're my partner. I should be able to trust you."

"You can trust me. I would not hurt you." The words were simple and sincere.

Chocolate brown looked into Cognac as Hanlan met Canin's eyes. Sincerity and a hint of something else, something that he couldn't name. Hanlan nodded, then dropped his eyes and took a sip of coffee. "I don't think the son did it."

"Any particular reason?"

Hanlan shook his head. "Just a gut feeling." He took another sip. "Julia Lupo and Jennifer Lowell are my top suspects. Either one could be the woman at Shaw's firm and both seem to have an interest in Raven Manor."

Canin tilted his head. "There's something else. What is it?"

"I don't like them." That was putting it mildly, but he didn't want to say he hated them. There was no logical reason to his deep hatred of them. They just felt evil to him.

"Neither of them have a charming personality," Canin said as if he at least half agreed.

"I want to look over Raven Manor before we release it. There is some reason both of them want that place."

"Is that why you signed out the keys on our way out? You want to go now?"

"No time like the present."

"I thought we were going to talk."

"We did." He was still wary, but he felt better about trusting Canin with his life.

Canin looked at him a moment before speaking. "You don't really trust anyone, do you? Who hurt you?"

Hanlan raised an eyebrow.

"You don't tell people what you're thinking. You

think they'll use it somehow against you. Someone had to have done it to you before and more than just once."

Hanlan looked away, then took a sip of coffee and stood.

Canin looked up at him for a moment, then stood as well. "I can take a hint. Let's go."

Turning, Hanlan headed for the car with Canin just behind him. They got into the car and Hanlan drove toward the Manor. The gate was open when they got there and Hanlan pulled up into the circular drive. He parked and they got out of the car. They headed for the front door as Hanlan retrieved the key from his jacket pocket. It required a little force to push the door open once Hanlan unlocked it but they entered and Hanlan closed the door behind them. With a flick of a switch the foyer lit up, chasing away the bit of shadow that had hovered there.

"Where do you want to start?" Canin asked, glancing around.

"The study." He put his words to action and went into that room. Pausing just inside, he glanced around before heading for the one wall of bookshelves. He began pulling the books out before putting them back in, hunting for a trigger. These bookshelves may hide a door.

"Ah." Canin started on the next set of shelves over.

They worked quietly for a while, then Hanlan knelt and pulled a book off the bottom shelve. There was a click, then the floor slid out from underneath Hanlan and he was falling.

He hit hard. Whatever he hit gave way a bit under him but softened his fall. He checked himself out as best he could before he tried to move. Nothing broken that he could tell.

The floor must have slid back because it was pitch black. No light anywhere.

His hand found his old lighter that he still carried though he had quit smoking years ago. It had been a gift and he had not wanted to part with it. He flicked the lighter and glanced around when it flared to life. It did not cast a large light but he could tell he was in a cell. He had fallen on a straw mattress in the center and the glint of the metal bars showed him which way was the front.

There was a shift in the air and a pair of red glowing eyes appeared on the other side of the bars. The creature paced just outside those bars and Hanlan could hear the sound of toe nails on the stone. Every now and then those eyes would stare directly at him and a growl would rumble across the air between them.

Hanlan remained kneeling on the mattress and watched, waiting. He knew if not for the bars he would have been torn apart.

Light suddenly rained down on him from above and he blinked as he was blinded. He could hear the creature move away.

"Hanlan?" Canin called as his head ducked down the hole above.

"I'm here." He closed the lighter and returned it to his pocket. "What took you so long?"

"Can you tell where you're at?" Canin seem to ignore his question as if it was rhetorical.

"The dungeons I'd say." Hanlan glanced up the long way to the hole, then looked toward the bars. There was a barred door with the key stuck in it. "The door's got a key. You have a flashlight?"

Canin dropped a small hand-sized light and Hanlan caught it. "You sure you don't want me to come down there?"

Actually Hanlan did want him down there in case he ran into the creature again, but he shook his head. "I'll find my way out."

"If you're sure," Canin said.

"I am." He made his voice firm. Crawling off the mattress took a moment, then he turned on the flashlight and shined it toward the door. The flashlight put out an amazing amount of light for its size. In a few steps he was at the door and opened it. When nothing jumped out of the shadows at him, he relaxed a bit and took a step out of the cell. Several feet in front of him a stairway led up and he took it, hugging the wall as it spiraled up.

A floor up was another cell and a branching tunnel. He figured he was on the first floor of the manor and this was a 'secret' passageway. Steps inside the left branch was another ascending winding stairway so Hanlan took the right branch. The narrow corridor led a winding path for a few meters, then a slender alcove appeared. Inside was a door but no handles that Hanlan could see.

The faint sound of toe nails on stone reached his ears and Hanlan began to search in earnest. He pushed on the door but it didn't budge, then ran his free hand along the edges. A growl sounded from just behind him when his fingers snagged and he stumbled forward as the door suddenly opened. He regained his balance and whirled but the door had shut behind him and all he saw was a wall.

His heart started to slow as the adrenaline rush subsided and he glanced around. He was in the dining room. The wall he faced was the back one. There were two doors, one no doubt to the kitchen while the other should open into the hall. Light switches were set next to both doors so he headed for one of the doors. He flipped the switches when he got there and turned around to study the room.

Bead board covered the bottom half of the walls while striped wallpaper covered the upper half. Both concealed the 'secret' door on the back wall quite well. The one side wall had a beautifully carved buffet along it that matched the large table and chairs in the center of the room. An eerie watercolor of the manor hung above the buffet while an oil painting of a family was on the back wall where the 'secret' door was.

Hanlan didn't want to go back into the passageway but they needed to know where it led and what it concealed. Perhaps if both he and Canin went together the creature would not appear. If nothing else their combined firepower should be able to stop it. He didn't think his thirty-eight alone would do much good.

Movement at the other door drew his attention.

Canin stood there. "I saw the light," he told Hanlan.

"We need to follow the passageway I found."

"Hmm." Canin seemed to sniff the air and frowned. "Can we eat lunch first? We can always come back afterwards."

"I am hungry." Hanlan made sure the small flashlight was off and slipped it into his pocket. He joined Canin at the other door, then followed him back down the hall toward the foyer. There was no hurry to search the passageway. Perhaps by the time they returned the creature would have disappeared. Not that he wished it loose. But vanished back from wherever it came from. That he could hope. After all he didn't think the dog catcher would have much luck and he didn't want a death on his conscious if he called them.

So lunch and then he and Canin would return and search the passageway. Hopefully the creature would be gone and they would find what makes this place so valuable to two strong and independent women that one or both of them would kill for it.

CHAPTER 15

Hanlan pulled into the circular drive at Raven Manor and parked before the door. They had eaten at a little restaurant that Hanlan knew of not far from here. Neither of them had talked much. Canin had seemed sunk as deep in his thoughts as Hanlan had been. Though Hanlan had tried to keep his thoughts away from what they might have to face in the passageway. He leaned over as much as he could and reached under his seat, pulling out a long mag light.

"Do you have another mag?" Canin asked him.

"There's a smaller one in the glove box," Hanlan told him as he check to see if his flashlight worked.

Canin retrieved the mag from the box, then checked it.

They got out of the car and went up to the door. Hanlan unlocked it and they entered, closing the door behind them. The foyer was lit but the hallway was dark.

"Didn't you leave the dining room light on?"

"Yesss."

"Maybe we should..."

"Let's go," Hanlan interrupted as he headed toward the dining room. He flicked on his mag light and kept a steady pace, even though he was worried about what they would find. Was the creature now loose in the Manor and ready to pounce or was the one who caused all this waiting for them in the dining room to finish the detectives off themselves?

Nothing leaped out of the shadows as they walked and they made it to the dining room without incident. Hanlan flipped on the light and the room lit up.

It was empty.

After he glanced around to ensure the room was indeed empty, Hanlan went to the painting on the back wall and searched for a latch or lever with his free hand.

Canin remained standing in the doorway, his face scrunched up like he smelled something bad. "Maybe we should wait until tomorrow and get some of the guys to help us."

"They got their own work to do." A few moments later, Hanlan felt an irregular spot on the frame and pushed it firmly, causing the wall to open. He took a step inside, then looked at Canin. "You coming?"

Canin stared at him for a minute, then joined him

at the opening. "I still think this is a bad idea."

"We need to see where this leads."

"I know." Canin switched on his flashlight. "Let's do this before I think better of it."

Both detectives stepped further into the passageway and the door closed behind them. Hanlan took the lead and headed down the close winding path. There were a few more alcoves that they passed before the passageway widened into a small room with a spiral stairway leading down. Two skeletons sat leaning against the bit of railing above the stair.

Hanlan shown his light over them, noting what remained of their clothing. These bones were what was left of the Cummings he believed. Why they hadn't found their way out he didn't know.

"The Cummings?" Canin asked.

"Their clothing would say so." Hanlan moved to the stairway and shown his flashlight down. The darkness swallowed the light. A shiver ran through him, but what emotion had caused it he didn't know. All he felt was anticipation. "Let's see where this leads."

Canin fell in step behind him as Hanlan went down the stairway. At the bottom both detectives stopped and splayed their lights around.

The room was large but only seven feet tall. Directly in front of them about twenty feet away they could see the side of a statue. Its head touched the ceiling and its arms were out stretched, holding out a tube over an altar. There were carvings along the other walls but the wall behind the statue was blank.

But Hanlan only paid the room itself fleeting attention because laying sprawled out in front of the altar were three skeletons. He had a feeling these were the workmen that had went missing back in the 1800's.

"We'll have to call CSU." There was reluctance—and a bit of reverence--in Canin's voice.

"Yes." Hanlan too was reluctant to disturb this place. It had the feel of a church. Perhaps the altar made him feel that way.

Whatever it was made them both retreat back up the stairs before Canin pulled out his cell phone. While Canin called CSU, Hanlan went over to the two skeletons leaning against the railing. What was holding them up he didn't know. He didn't think their clothing alone would do it, especially not their skulls. But they were both sitting upright with bowed heads against the railing. Hanlan saw a flashlight in the one skeleton's lap which made no sense. Why hadn't they found a way out?

"They said they'd be here in twenty minutes." Canin moved his own light onto the skeleton couple. "They must have found one of the 'secret' doors."

"Yes, but why didn't they find their way out?"

"We may never know." He turned and took a step toward the passageway. "We need to go if we want to meet CSU when they get here."

"Yes." Hanlan moved away from the skeletons and headed into the passageway. "The other two people who disappeared must be here somewhere too."

"Maybe."

Hanlan led the way back to the alcove they entered by and opened the door. Both of them stepped out and Canin used a chair to block the door open. He headed for the front door while Hanlan waited in the dining room.

At least two of the disappearances were now explained, at least as to where they disappeared to and the how. Though Hanlan still couldn't fathom why the Cummings at least hadn't gotten out.

Canin appeared with two techs. As the techs set down their equipment, Canin looked at Hanlan. "I called the M.E. office. They'll be here in half an hour."

Hanlan nodded, then turned his attention to the techs. He told them about the passageway and where he and Canin had found the bodies. "There should be two more bodies in there somewhere," he added.

The techs nodded and disappeared into the passageway with the smaller suitcases from their trolleys of equipment.

"We waiting for the M.E.?" Canin asked.

"Yes." Hanlan suspected Brennon would beat the van here. She had an interest in this place and these bodies. He set his flashlight on the table and sat in one of the chairs to wait while Canin moved to the hall door so he could look down it toward the foyer.

Less than ten minutes later, Canin straightened and Brennon came flying through the doorway.

"You found them?" she demanded of Hanlan.

"The Cummings and the workmen from the 1800's but the two electricians are still missing."

"Huh." She peered at the open door to the passageway. "They were here all this time."

"Are you going to do the examinations?"

"No." She shook her head. "I don't do bones. Charles will do it."

"Charles?"

"Dr. Charles Jefferson. He's the city's Anthropologist."

"Did I hear my name?" An older man stepped into the dining room from the hall. "Brennon, what are you doing here?"

"Just to observe, Charles. I swear." She put up her hands.

The salt-n-pepper haired man looked at her over his glasses, then nodded before turning his attention to Hanlan. "You found the skeletons?"

"Yes." Hanlan stood and grabbed the mag light." I'll lead you to them."

"Good." Jefferson nodded. "When the morgue assistants get here send them along, would you?" he said to Canin before moving to the passageway door.

Hanlan slipped past him and flicked on the flashlight before heading down the narrow path with Jefferson and Brennon just behind him. The detective silently led the anthropologist and M.E. through the equally quiet passageway. He didn't feel the need to speak and the anthropologist didn't ask any questions.

Jefferson flipped on his own light when they got to the stairway area and moved toward the bones, leaving Hanlan and Brennon standing at the opening watching. The anthropologist knelt before the skeletons and ran his flashlight over them. "This is how you found them?"

"Yes."

"Hmm." He reached out a hand but before he could touch anything, the skeletons suddenly collapsed. Freezing, Jefferson stared at the now jumbled pile of bones. "Interesting."

Before Hanlan or Brennon could say anything, a CSU tech came up the stair. He stopped when he saw the other three.

"Ah the vibrations from his steps must have caused the collapse," Jefferson said as he stood.

"Then why didn't they fall when Canin and I went up and down the stairs?" Hanlan countered.

Jefferson didn't answer.

"This place has an interesting history, as you well know, Charles," Brennon said.

Charles snorted. "Poppycock."

"Well, I'm done downstairs," the CSU tech said. "Not much evidence to gather. Make sure the remnants of clothing is sent to us after they're removed from the bones."

"We will," Jefferson promised.

"Where's your partner?" Hanlan asked.

"He headed the other way. Which is where I am headed now." The tech nodded to them all, then went back into the passageway.

Hanlan had a twinge of conscious about letting the techs wander the passageway where he had run into a dangerous creature, but something told him it was long gone. He shoved the feeling aside and moved to the stairway. "The other three are downstairs," he told the other two before heading down.

"My God," Brennon whispered.

The CSU tech had left a small lantern on the altar. Its light showed the bones and the statue clearly but faded just beyond, giving the room a sense of vastness.

Jefferson moved to the area in front of the altar and knelt, keeping his free hand away from the bones.

"Looks to me like they were knocked down and killed where they fell. What do you think?" Hanlan asked him.

"I don't speculate." Jefferson stood.

"What can you say?"

"They didn't die from asphyxiation or naturally."

"What about the ones upstairs?"

"Starvation or dehydration could have killed them. I didn't see any trauma to the bones in either of them."

"So you see some with these bones?"

"I'm not going to speculate," he repeated.

"Make sure you send a copy of your report to me. Detective Hanlan. Fifteenth precinct."

Jefferson nodded.

"Hanlan?" Canin's voice called from upstairs.

"We're here," he called up before telling Jefferson, "Your morgue assistants must be here."

They all headed up the stairs to find two morgue assistants and Canin filling half the stair area with two body bags. Jefferson directed the morgue assistants to the bones as Hanlan, Brennon, and Canin moved toward the passageway. The three of them headed back to the dining room exit, leaving the others to their work.

CHAPTER 16

Back at the dining room, Hanlan, Canin and Brennon ran into the CSU techs. They were packing up their gear.

"Done already?" Hanlan asked.

"Not much to gather after all these years," the one they had met at the stairway said. "Oh, Roger found your other two missings. They're on the second floor at the foot of an ascending stairway that leads to the attic. It looks like they fell down the stairs and died."

Hanlan and Canin looked at each other.

"If you're going, I am too," Brennon said.

"Someone needs to tell Dr. Jefferson." Hanlan looked at her.

"I'll go, "the tech who spoke before said. "I don't

mind."

"Okay." Hanlan led the way back in the passageway and turned the opposite way toward the cells this time, Canin and Brennon right behind him. He retraced his earlier steps to the top cell and went up the stairway in the left tunnel opening.

At the top of the stair a winding path led away and they followed it, passing alcoves as they went. Finally, it opened up into a small area with an ascending stairway. Hanlan's and Canin's lights lit up the area at the bottom of the stairs. Bones littered the bottom steps and the stone before it. It did indeed look like they had fallen and died there.

"Feet away from freedom," Brennon murmured.

Hanlan ascended the stairway carefully. It ended at a trapdoor and Hanlan pushed it up. He had to put some muscle into it but it opened. His light revealed what indeed looked like an attic and he let the door close. Moving just as carefully as he had up, he headed down and rejoined the other two at the bottom of the stairway.

"Anything?" Canin asked.

"No." Hanlan shook his head even though he knew Canin probably wouldn't see it. "Looks like they fell."

"Both of them?" Canin asked a little skeptically.

"Not impossible," Brennon said.

"We may never know." Hanlan looked at the bones one last time, then headed for the passageway. "We'd best get back to the station and update the Captain."

"Yes." Canin agreed as he and Brennon fell in step behind Hanlan.

The three of them made it back to the dining room exit before running into Jefferson and the two morgue assistants. They exchanged a nod and places with each other before the anthropologist and the assistants headed down the passageway towards the cells.

"You going back to work?" Hanlan asked Brennon as they left the dining room, going toward the foyer.

"Yes. I have two more autopsies to do before I leave for the evening."

They made the foyer and parted ways at the door. Brennon to her car and the detectives to theirs. Hanlan slid into the driver's seat as Canin got in the passenger side. The flashlights went back to their places, then Hanlan drove around the drive and out the gate, heading back to the station.

"You want me to update the notes while you talk to the Captain?" Canin asked.

"That would be the best division of labor."

Canin looked at him. "Are you mocking me?"

Hanlan didn't answer as he continued to drive.

They rode the rest of the way in silence. Once behind the building Hanlan parked and both detectives exited the car. It only took them a few minutes to make it upstairs and into the bullpen. Canin stopped at his desk, but Hanlan continued on to the captain's office.

The captain looked up when he stopped in her doorway. "Detective?"

Hanlan proceeded to tell her what they found at Raven Manor and a basic rundown of the disappearances as Brennon had told him. "I told Dr.

Jefferson to send a copy of his reports to me," he added after he finished.

"You found nothing to explain the interest shown by Ms. Lupo and Professor Lowell?" She asked after a moment of silence.

"Nothing so far. But I plan to return tomorrow."

"It will have to be in the afternoon. The One-Eight visited Professor Lowell this afternoon. She and her lawyer will be here tomorrow at ten."

"She's said that before."

"If she doesn't show this time she'll go to jail and the University will fire her."

Hanlan raised an eyebrow.

"I have my ways." The captain smiled. "Now go. We both have work to do before we call it a day."

"Yes, ma'am." Hanlan gave her a little salute and headed back to his desk. He fell into his chair with a tired sigh and looked at Canin. "You nearly done?"

"Just about." He paused and looked at Hanlan. "Do we really have to do the reports on finding the bones?"

"The Cummings' at least." Hanlan affirmed. He scooted up to his computer and started typing. "We closed the case or at least will close it once Dr. Jefferson's report is done so we have to finish the paperwork." At Canin's moan Hanlan smiled. "Don't worry. I'll do it. I'm doing it right now as a matter of fact."

Canin gave a sigh of relief, then scooted back from his computer. "Done! I think I deserve a cup of coffee."

"Not from the break room, you don't," Hanlan told him. "That tar will melt your stomach lining if you actually swallow it. Most spit it back out as soon as it hits their tongue. We bring our own in. Why do you think I get a coffee to go at lunch if I know we're coming back here?"

"I was hoping Homicide had better coffee." Canin slumped in his chair. "I love coffee."

"The captain said Lowell is supposedly coming in tomorrow morning at ten. With her lawyer."

"You want to bet on whether or not she'll come in this time?"

"The captain made consequences if she doesn't." Hanlan scooted back from his computer. "That will do until we get Dr. Jefferson's report." He looked at Canin. "You want to go to Joey's for coffee?"

Before Canin could say anything, his cell phone rang. He held up his finger to Hanlan to wait and answered with "Canin." A frown settled on his face as he listened, then he said, "Alright." before slipping the phone back in his jacket. "Someone wants to meet you," he told Hanlan.

Hanlan raised an eyebrow.

"I can't tell you any more right now." Canin stood. "Just trust me for a bit."

Hanlan looked at him for a moment, then stood. "Don't make me regret this."

"I won't." His tone was serious and his eyes were sincere.

Hanlan nodded and followed Canin out of the bullpen to the elevator. They rode down in silence. Hanlan took the lead to the car and they got in as soon as they reached it. "Where are we going? "he asked Canin as he started the vehicle.

"Halston Park."

That park was near the park they were in earlier today. It was mainly used as a dog park for the aspiring wealthy. Hanlan frowned and drove out of the lot. It was also known as for its bad night life. He glanced at the darkening sky. Night came earlier and earlier as the season began to change.

It didn't take long for them to arrive at the park. Once Hanlan parked, they got out and Canin led the way toward a stand of trees along the north edge of the park. The area seemed empty but for them, yet Hanlan's hair on the back of his neck was standing up. Something awaited them in the trees and it didn't feel human.

A few yards from the stand, a blur shot out of the trees and something knocked Hanlan down. Pain stabbed through his head as he hit the ground but he managed to keep his eyes open.

The giant gray wolf stood over him, its fangs gleaming.

There was a flash and the black wolf suddenly slammed into the gray wolf, forcing it away from Hanlan. The detective raised his head to follow them as they squared off at each other.

"Atch!" a harsh voice barked.

The two wolves froze, then back away from each other as an old man came out of the trees. He was dressed in linen pants and a colorful peasant shirt.

Roma.

Pain stabbed through Hanlan's head again as memories of his great grandmother shot through his mind. He laid his head back on the ground and closed his eyes, overwhelmed. The old man continued to talk in Romani at the two wolves who stood like chastised children but Hanlan only caught a few words. He had only a child's vocabulary anyway.

His great grandmother's stories were coming back to him. The Del Mulanti Ruv. The Shilmulo. Her stories were couched in a way that an eight year old would understand. Roma fairy tales. How much was true he didn't know. But he had loved the scary stories more.

"Detective." The old man's voice was unaccented and close.

Hanlan opened his eyes to see the old man squatting beside him. He could see the two wolves out of the corner of his eye, but he kept his attention on the old man. There was a feeling of power radiating from him. This old man was an alpha male.

"I apologize for her attack. Had I known her intentions I would have sent her away as soon as I sensed her enter the woods." The old man helped Hanlan to sit up. "I am Phuro."

"Elder." Hanlan was sure that was not his real name. But he didn't blame the old man for not trusting him.

"Yes." Phuro stood and reached his hand down to Hanlan.

Taking the hand, Hanlan allowed the old man to help him to his feet. Once he was steady he withdrew his hand and glanced around. There were only the two of them and the wolves. Hanlan felt sure the black wolf was Canin. But which of the two female suspects was the gray?

Or …

He could sense that this was not the same gray that had attacked him before. The feeling was not logical but there was just something different about this wolf. Were both women Shilmulo? It would explain his instant dislike (hatred) of them.

"I must say you are taking this quite well," the old man told Hanlan.

"I'm sure I'll have a serious mental breakdown later." Hanlan paused. "So miri Bunica's stories were true. The Del Mulanti Ruv exist."

"That is what our Chosen called us."

"Spirit ghostwolves. She also told of those that went bad, the Shilmulo."

"Yes, power can corrupt if one's will is not strong enough."

"You may be Del Mulanti Ruv but she is Shilmulo." Hanlan pointed at the gray. "Can you not tell?"

"Dook," the old man whispered. "The sight."

The gray made a choking sound and whirled, disappearing into the trees seconds later.

A shimmer and Canin was back in human form.

"Permission is granted, young one," the old man told Canin. "Though I have a feeling he knows more than you about some things."

"Thank you, Elder."

"Permission for what?" Hanlan asked.

"To tell you about the Del Mulanti Ruv and some of my secrets," Canin told him. "That is what you wanted, isn't it?"

The old man laughed. "Be careful of this one, my son. He already has you wrapped around his finger."

"What is he talking about?" Hanlan demanded of Canin as the old man headed back into the trees.

"One of those secrets I have to tell you about." Canin rubbed his neck with a sheepish look on his face. "Let's head to your apartment and we can talk."

Hanlan narrowed his eyes at Canin suspiciously but followed him back toward the car. They would indeed talk.

CHAPTER 17

The detectives made a detour through a drive-thru before they headed for Hanlan's apartment. Hanlan wasn't really hungry but he could always have it for breakfast if he didn't eat it tonight. He was more interested in what Canin was going to tell him. Was what his great grandmother had told him as a child the truth couched in fairy tales?

Hanlan pulled into his parking slot and grabbed the food before they both got out.

Red eyes glared at them as a growl came from the shadows. A gray wolf crept out and crouched as if to pounce on them.

Canin took a few steps forward so he was between Hanlan and the wolf but he did not change forms. He merely stared into the gray's eyes.

A brown and white wolf took a step out of the shadows and barked at the gray. When the gray did not react, it took another step and barked again. The gray stood slowly, then turned away from the two detectives before disappearing back into the shadows. With a huff, the brown and white wolf turned and followed the gray into the darkness.

"She is definitely Shilmulo," Hanlan told Canin. "The other is borderline, but this one is firmly in vampire territory. She would have killed us both with no hesitation. She only backed down because she didn't know if she could take both you and the other out without her getting seriously hurt."

"Yes. That's the way I saw it as well."

"Can you tell which one it was?"

"No. My senses are limited in this form. They are heightened but not to that degree. And I have never met either of them formally in wolf form."

"Let's head inside before she decides to return." Hanlan nodded toward his door.

"Yes." Canin followed Hanlan to the door, then inside, making sure the door was locked behind them. "Are you hungry?" he asked, gesturing to the bag of food.

"Not really." Hanlan put the bag in the refrigerator, then poured himself a shot of whiskey which he immediately drank. "Okay. The living room."

They went into the living area and Hanlan sat on the couch while Canin chose the chair beside it.

"How much do you know of the Del Mulanti Ruv?" Canin asked.

"Assume I know nothing," Hanlan told him.

Canin grinned.

Hanlan rolled his eyes.

"Okay." Canin turned serious. "Our origins were lost in the shrouds of time so I can't tell you how we came to be. We just always were. Though we are loosely associated into Packs, we are actually lone creatures. Packs have territories and a hierarchy."

"The old man is the alpha male for this territory?"

"For the City, yes."

"And what about the Shilmulo?"

"The werewolf and vampire legends were based on the Shilmulo, those who lost themselves to the dark side."

"The old man said if their will was weak they became vampires."

"Though we are not immortal we do live a long time, centuries, and we can lose our way if we give in to the loneliness and other emotions that can engulf us if we don't find our companion."

"Companion or--mate?"

"Companion. There is nothing sexual in the companion bond. It's too intimate for that."

Hanlan raised an eyebrow.

"With humans everything is about sex. Cuddling and touch is not only for that, but for comfort and warmth. I joined the Force because it had a similarity to what the companion bond offers."

"Brotherhood."

"Yes."

Hanlan digested that for a moment before asking, "Is that what the old man was talking about at the end?"

Canin shifted, the sheepish look back on his face, before he nodded.

"When did you know?"

"The second I shook your hand."

Hanlan swept a hand over his face, closing his eyes.

"That night I spoke to the Elder."

"Those plans you mentioned."

"Yes."

Sighing, Hanlan opened his eyes and looked at Canin. He really needed to have a breakdown but he also had to understand. "That evening I was attacked, you were stalking me?"

"Not stalking. Watching out for you. I suspected Lupo would pay you a visit sometime and I was worried Lowell might as well."

"So you were working with me during the day and guarding me at night. When did you sleep?"

"Catnaps during the night."

Hanlan rubbed his face again.

"How about I explain the advantages of being a companion?"

"Sure."

"Your aging slows down to match your Ruv as long as your Ruv lives. You heal faster and common cold and viruses don't affect you. Your reflexes are better. And best of all, no more thinning hair."

Hanlan looked at Canin. He knew Canin was trying to lighten the mood, but he didn't feel amused.

"Truth." Canin held his hand up in the boy scout

gesture.

"Explain more about this companion business. Like what's involved." Nothing is for free or without consequences. Hanlan had learned that the hard way.

"I don't understand what you mean."

"What do I have to do or you have to do?"

"The bonding, you mean."

"Yes." If the consequences that could result were too high, he would pass. Get a new partner.

In a blink of his eye the black wolf was crowding Hanlan. It grabbed his wrist in its mouth and bit down, drawing blood.

Hanlan sat still until it let go of his wrist, then he scooted away. Heat was spreading from the bite marks but he was suddenly shaking from the cold that was now racking his body. He tried to get up, but his body did nothing but shiver.

A shimmer and Canin was kneeling beside him. "I'm sorry, but I could sense you were withdrawing. Once we meet our companion we are compelled to bond with them. The longer the time we're not, the stronger the compulsion. I almost bit you the night of the attack." He made Hanlan more comfortable on the couch, then spread the throw from its back over Hanlan. "We'll be bonded by morning. Just stop fighting and go to sleep."

Hanlan tried to move again, but his body was locked into shivers. Where the warmth from the bite marks spread, his body relaxed but he still couldn't get up. His thoughts grew sluggish and sleep called him, but he wasn't sure he wanted to follow it.

Canin sat on the couch beside him and ran his

hand through Hanlan's hair. "Just sleep and you can yell at me in the morning."

His great grandmother's voice drifted through Hanlan's mind. She was telling one of her stories. He was in bed sick and she was sitting next to him, waving her hands as she spoke. The scene was clear in his mind and he drifted off to sleep, listening to her tell her tale.

CHAPTER 18

A cold nose in his face woke Hanlan.

Cognac eyes stared back at him from a foot away.

Memory made him jerk up right and glare at the black wolf. "We need to talk."

The wolf huffed and jumped onto a chair. A shimmer and Canin was sitting in the chair wearing a different suit than yesterday.

"How did you...Never mind. That was not good what you did last night."

"I don't regret it," Canin told him. "You were getting cold feet, letting the past interfere with your mind. I am not whomever it was that hurt you."

"You hurt me last night!" In more ways than one.

"I am sorry, but I don't regret it," Canin repeated.

Hanlan scrubbed his face, then ran his fingers through his hair. He could actually feel what Canin was feeling. It tugged at the edges of his mind. The feel of it was similar to what he felt when his gut told him things. His great grandmother and the old man both called it Dook, the sight, but it was actually feelings. "It was still not good."

"I apologize for how it happened but not that it did."

"What now?"

"Now you hurry up and shower and change clothes or we'll be late."

"You know that's not what I meant." Hanlan glared at him.

"We'll talk after work tonight."

Hanlan looked at Canin who met his eyes. Sincerity shown there and he could feel it as well so he nodded and got off the couch. He rush through his shower and put on a blue suit. Looking into the mirror, he paused. Normally he'd have a five o'clock shadow but his face looked clean-shaven, though he could feel a bit of stubble and a few of his wrinkles had disappeared. He still looked his age but there was something ethereal about him now. Giving himself one last look, he headed back into the living room.

Canin held out a cup of coffee and a warmed breakfast burrito he must have gotten from Hanlan's freezer. "I already had mine."

The detective accepted them both and scarfed down the burrito. He savored the coffee for a moment before finishing it and setting the cup down.

Both of them headed out the door and got into the car. They rode in silence to the station, each content in the quiet. Once at the station it was only a matter of minutes before they were in the bullpen at their desks.

There was a new folder in Hanlan's in-box so he picked it up and flipped it open. "This is the Lab results from the Shaw case. Same DNA anomaly that was in the Graves'. The hairs found on Shaw's body came back Canis Lupus, wolf hair. And the shoe print came back to a ladies wedge size 9."

"They found a shoe print? And how do they know it's the killer's?"

"Next to the body in the bit of blood, it says here." Hanlan tapped the folder.

"I wonder what size Professor Lowell wears because I don't see Ms. Lupo in wedges."

"Neither do I. Stilettos, but not wedges." Hanlan closed the folder and laid it on his desk. "However we can't dismiss her."

"I know. You going to ask the Captain for a warrant?"

"For both. Maybe Howell and Deneque can serve the warrant on Ms. Lupo for us." Hanlan stood and headed to the captain's office. He stopped in the doorway and cleared his throat. "Captain?"

She set the letter she was reading down and looked at him. "Need something, Detective?"

"Warrants for Ms. Lupo's and Professor Lowell's shoes. CSU found a bloody ladies shoe print at the Shaw scene. Be nice to have it by the time Lowell shows up."

The captain looked at him a moment, then nodded. "I'll see what I can do."

"Thank you, Captain." He turned to go, but stopped when the captain spoke again.

"Is the case getting less complicated, detective?"

"Marginally."

"Then keep at it."

"Yes, ma'am." Hanlan headed back to his desk and slumped into his chair. He still had questions, but he might never get them answered before he solved the case.

"Well?"

"We'll see." He picked up his phone and punched in a number with one hand while bringing it to his ear with the other. "Howell, Hanlan. Think you can do me a favor?" He paused. "We're waiting on a warrant to collect Ms. Lupo's shoes. If you could execute it when it comes in, I'd be grateful." Another pause. "Good. I'll buy you and Deneque a beer." He hung up the phone, then looked at Canin. "They're at loose ends right now with the court so they'll do it."

"Good."

"Is there anything I should know about Ms. Lupo or Professor Lowell?"

"I have never met them before this case."

"You said something about not formally meeting them so I thought you might have met them informally."

"I am not a formal member of the city's Pack," Canin said in a low voice. "You would say I'm an associate member."

"We are definitely having that talk later."

Canin dipped his head in acknowledgment. "You want me to do the notes?" he asked after a moment of silence. "I've learned to edit creatively on reports."

"Go for it." Hanlan leaned back in his chair. He felt good. No little aches or pains that had crept up on him through the years. His body felt lighter, looser, than it had in a long time. Physically this bonding was good for him. He wonder though what the Ruv got out of the deal besides companionship. That seemed a small return.

Canin raised his eyes from the computer and met Hanlan's. He held Hanlan's eyes for a long moment, then turned his attention back to the screen. Contentment radiated from him.

Hanlan was unsure what he himself felt. Too much conflicting emotions and no time to process left him uncertain of his own mind.

The captain appeared right then and Hanlan straightened in his chair as she held out two warrants. He took them and she whirled, heading back to her office without a word.

This case was obviously wearing on everybody.

Howell and Deneque showed up seconds later. "Saw the captain," Howell said as they reached Hanlan's desk.

Hanlan glanced at the warrants, then handed one to Howell. "Be careful."

Both detectives nodded, then headed for the front doors.

"You think she'll comply without a fuss." Canin's tone made it a statement.

"Ms. Lupo struck me as a practical person.

Lowell on the other hand is impulsive, passionate. She's going to give a fuss."

"You think Professor Lowell is the killer." Again a statement.

"Without evidence it doesn't matter what I think." His phone rang just then and he answered with "Hanlan." He listened for a moment then said, "Bring them up. Interview Room 2." Hanging up, he looked at Canin. "Professor Lowell and her lawyer are here."

"The lawyer might be the Pack's legal counsel." He kept his voice low. "I met one of them when I moved here but not the main one."

Hanlan nodded acknowledgment. He saw the captain leave her office and head toward the interview rooms. They were going to have an audience so he had to be careful with what he said and how he said it. The lawyer he didn't care about but he did about the captain. He caught sight of the officer leading Lowell and an older man toward the interview room and turned his attention back to Canin. "The captain's in the observation room."

Canin frowned as he nodded his understanding.

Hanlan picked up the warrant and slipped it into his jacket pocket. "Let's get this started."

Both detectives stood and headed back to the interview rooms. They nodded to the officer as he left and continued into the room, closing the door behind them. The lawyer and Lowell were just sitting down facing the mirror so the detectives moved to the other chairs. Hanlan sat down but Canin remained standing leaning against the mirror with his arms crossed.

"Thank you for coming in, Professor Lowell," Hanlan said, his tone suspiciously bland.

"Like I had a choice," she growled back at him.

"Jennifer," the lawyer said in a warning tone. "I'm Charles Townsen, Professor Lowell's attorney. You wanted to ask her about the murders of Mr. and Mrs. Graves and Mr. Shaw so ask."

"Where were you Monday afternoon between 5 pm and 6:30?"

"In the University library researching." She was glaring at him as she spoke.

"Can anyone verify that?"

"I was alone in a study room." Her tone was defiant.

"Do you have to sign in or sign out a key or anything?"

"No. I have that time permanently three days a week."

"And Tuesday around the same time?"

"The library."

"So no one can verify that either?"

"Detective, she's co-operating. No need to get sarcastic." Townsen tsk-tsked.

"We get suspicious when people run from us."

"Run? She's here."

"Now. But she missed her other appointment."

The lawyer raised an eyebrow and Hanlan suspected Lowell hadn't told Townsen about that. "Is that all, Detective?"

"No." He looked back at Lowell. "What is so special about Raven Manor to cause all this?"

She stared at him for a long moment, so long that Hanlan didn't think she would answer, before she spoke. "You should ask Phuro about the alternate history of that place. It holds many secrets." She stood and looked at the lawyer. "We're done here."

"Before you go," Hanlan said as he pulled out the warrant. "I need your shoes."

Anger swept across Lowell's face, eyes blazing red for a second.

Townsen gripped her arm, his knuckles white with the pressure he was exerting. "Jennifer," he warned.

She jerked her arm away and sat down to take her shoes off, her movements tense with her anger. The shoes were thrown on the table before she stood and stalked out of the room.

"Tell her our colleagues will be by to get the rest of her shoes later," Hanlan told the lawyer as Townsen stood.

"I would advise you to stay away from her, Detective, but I know you can't as you're the lead detective. However it would be best if you're not alone with her."

"Hadn't planned on it."

"Good. Good Day, Detectives." The lawyer gave them both a nod and left the room.

Hanlan stood, but before he could say or do anything the captain appeared in the doorway.

"Who's this Phuro?" she demanded. "Your notes don't mention this person."

Canin straightened and moved to stand next to Hanlan. "An historian with the Alsena Historical Society and Trust. They were helping the Graves research Raven Manor's history. I didn't think it relevant but if you want I can amend the notes."

"No." She shook her head, then sighed. "Sorry. I had another meeting with the Brass. An early lunch sounds good. Carry on."

The detectives watched her turn and walk away.

"I agree. An early lunch does sound good. And you can give Phuro a call while we're gone." Hanlan shoved the warrant back into his jacket pocket and headed for the door.

Canin nodded and followed Hanlan out.

CHAPTER 19

Lunch was at a corner in Joey's so Canin could make his phone call in relative privacy. Phuro had agreed to a meeting and surprisingly at his office in the Trust's main building. So they didn't head right back to the precinct after lunch but to Phuro's office.

The Alsena Historical Society and Trust was headquartered in the One-Eight's area in what used to be a library. It's brick and mortar facade was as impressive and clean as the day it was built. The Trust took care of its buildings very well.

Hanlan pulled into its parking lot and found a slot near its doors. He and Canin got out and headed up the short stairway to the carved doors. They entered and paused just inside.

Catwalks and stairs wove through the cathedral like room. Everything was wood and glass wherever they looked. Where shelves had once been on the three floors there appeared to be small rooms and hallways. A wooden small desk was set to the right and a woman was headed their way from it .

"It is impressive the first time you see it," the woman said with a smile. "I'm Beth. How may I help you?"

"They're here to see me, Beth," Phuro said as he came up to them. "We're going to use one of the conference rooms if that is alright?"

"Sure, Professor Ulven. The Canid room is open."

"Thank you, my dear." He motioned for the two detectives to follow him and headed toward a hallway to the right. Walking briskly, Phuro led them down the hallway to a door with a plaque reading 'Canid'. He hustled them inside and closed the door behind them all. A small oval table dominated the room with a stuffed wolf laying in its center and he gestured for them to take a seat at one of the wooden chairs. "This is my favorite room besides my office."

Hanlan grunted as he sat in a chair. He wasn't in the mood for small talk.

Canin sat beside Hanlan and Phuro took a chair across from them before he looked at the detectives. "Raven Manor has many secrets. To begin with it was originally called Ruven Manor and it's from Romania, not England. The company that moved it was from England, though the engineer was actually Scottish."

"The engineer that disappeared while reconstructing the place and we subsequently found?"

"Yes." Phuro nodded. "He was probably too nosy for his own good."

"Why was it moved?"

"We don't know. We just know it was and that it's family disappeared."

"Ms. Lupo said its her 'ancestral' home."

"She is distantly related to the original family but so are several others."

"Why is she and Lowell so keen on getting control of the place?"

"That's where the legend comes in." Phuro leaned forward, his elbows on the table and his head resting on his entwined hands. "The Lexicon Codex."

"You telling me they believe that old myth?" Canin asked, incredulously.

"It's not a myth."

"What?"

"Could you tell me what you're talking about here?" Hanlan interjected.

"The Codex is our version of the Bible," Canin said.

"It's more than that," Phuro chided. "Whomever possesses it is said to be able to rule the world, humans and Del Mulanti Ruv."

"And what does Raven Manor have to do with it?"

"Its family were supposedly the Codex's caretakers, keeping it safe from Shilmulo and humans alike. The legend says that the Codex is hidden in the Manor and the only clue to its whereabouts is two words—The inscription."

"There's plenty of inscriptions in that underground room with the altar," Hanlan said. Something tugged at his memory. "The altar itself even had one."

"Probably a blessing," Phuro said.

"Maybe." But Hanlan didn't think so. He would have to visit that room again with Canin to translate. "So this legend is why one or both of them are killing people?"

"If they have truly become Shilmulo then yes." Phuro answered him. "Vampires rarely need reasons to kill, any excuse will do. I will have to speak with my enforcers."

"Enforcers?"

"One or both of them have gone Rogue and are jeopardizing the security of the rest of my Pack. I can't allow that."

Hanlan frowned. He didn't like the sound of that.

"Like you I have a responsibility to keep my people safe. We police our own." Phuro stood. "I'll escort you out."

Canin stood and Hanlan reluctantly got up as well. The detectives followed Phuro back to the front doors where he left them without a word. Both of them went through the doors and down the stairs in silence. Once at the car, Hanlan slid into the driver's seat while Canin got in the passenger side.

Hanlan drove out of the parking lot and headed toward the station. He glanced over at Canin. "Were you an Enforcer?"

"Yes."

Canin's tone hadn't invited questions but Hanlan still asked, "Is this something we're going to talk about?"

"Eventually."

Hanlan left it at that.

They made good time to the station and Hanlan parked in his usual spot behind the building. Both got out and hurried upstairs to the bullpen. Howell and Deneque should be back by now and they wanted to get the scoop first hand. The other two detectives were just returning to the bullpen themselves when Hanlan and Canin walked in.

Hanlan stopped the two of them and pulled out the other warrant. "How would you like to earn two more beers?"

Before he had even finished talking, Deneque snatched the warrant from his hand.

"Take some uniforms with you this time," Hanlan told them as they turned to go. "You may have to restrain her."

"She's a professor," Deneque said as he and his partner looked at Hanlan.

"Suspected of three violent murders," Hanlan returned. "And she's got a temper."

Howell nodded and dragged his partner out the door while Hanlan and Canin continued on to their desks.

"You do a little more creative writing on the notes," Hanlan told Canin.

Canin nodded as he sat down and rolled up to the computer. "What are you going to be doing?" he asked as he started typing.

"If I'm not mistaken," Hanlan said as he picked

up the large envelope in his in-box. "This is Dr. Jefferson's preliminary report." He sat down and opened the envelope , pulling out a thick report seconds later. The envelope was tossed on the desk, then Hanlan started reading. After a few minutes, he flipped through the rest of the report. "The Doc must have worked through the night," he commented as he went back to the first page. "This is pretty detailed."

"What's his verdict?"

"The Cummings is inconclusive. No abnormalities. No broken bones. Nothing. It's as if they just sat down and died."

"So hunger and thirst?"

"That's his surmise. But he has unknown as the cause and manner." He laid the report on his desk and turned to his computer.

"What about the three in the crypt?"

"He surmises that their throats were ripped out and dropped beside them after a struggle. The position of the bodies themselves and the location of the hyoid bone led him to that conclusion. However all he can really state for sure is that the hyoid bone was removed and dropped beside the bodies. He found some fractures but they weren't enough to cause death."

"They probably were too nosy for their own good."

Hanlan frowned and looked at him as he paused in his own typing.

"Personal crypts are just that—personal. They shouldn't have went down there, especially if they didn't have permission."

"They were probably just curious as they had probably help put it up. They were after all the workers who did that."

"We must remain in secret," Canin said in a low voice. "The wrong kind of attention can be deadly for us."

Hanlan returned to his typing but he continued to frown. His phone rang and he answered with "Hanlan." There was a pause, then he said, "Thank you for the information." He hung up and returned to his typing. "That was Ms Young, Stephen Shaw's secretary. Robert Shaw's funeral is tomorrow at 1 pm."

"We going?" Canin asked as he returned to his own typing.

"Yes."

"It's not at Ballday's, is it?"

Hanlan flashed him a smile. "Harlin Cemetery. Didn't you like Ballday's?"

"No," was the short answer back.

Hanlan laughed, humor restored. He scooted away from his computer and leaned back in his chair. "Are you up for a little excursion at Raven Manor before we go to the funeral tomorrow?" He wanted to test his theory but he wanted their talk too.

Canin rolled away from his computer and looked at Hanlan, raising an eyebrow.

"I have an idea about that inscription bit and I need a translator."

"When do you want to go?"

"Tomorrow morning is soon enough. We have that talk we need to do tonight."

"What did the good Doctor say about the two on the stairway?" Canin asked, changing the subject. "A fall like we thought?"

"He thinks they had help but that's only his opinion. The injuries to the bones are consistent with a fall for both, but he says the odds of both of them falling are astronomical. However, it's not impossible."

Before Canin or Hanlan could say anything more, Howell and Deneque came up to Hanlan's desk. "The One-Eight obliged us with uniforms and thank you for the suggestion," Howell said, the spokesman as always for the partners.

Hanlan raised an eyebrow.

"I swear she was growling at us the whole time we were there. If we had been alone I think she would have attacked us."

"All the shoes with the Lab now?" Hanlan asked.

"Yes." Howell nodded. "We're going to call it quits for the day. We got the shift this weekend."

"We're about ready to head out too," Hanlan told them. "Shaw's funeral is tomorrow."

"Well, good luck." Both of the other detectives gave a little wave as they headed back toward the front doors.

"You done with the notes?" Hanlan asked Canin.

"Yes."

"I wrote a progress report on the Cummings case. Once we get the official report we can officially close it." Hanlan stood and pushed his chair under his desk. "Let's get out of here before something else comes up. Like the Captain wanting a progress report."

Canin nodded and stood, pushing his chair under his desk before he and Hanlan headed out of the bullpen.

Supper consisted of the food they had bought the other night. They had reheated it in Hanlan's microwave and ate in the living room. Their trash was picked up and they were both settled back in the living room with a beer.

Silence reigned for a moment before Canin spoke. "I don't know how to start. Perhaps you should ask me some questions."

"I don't know where to start." And Hanlan didn't. He had so many questions. And he wanted to understand. The Del Mulanti Ruv seem to have a whole different outlook that made him uneasy because he didn't understand their culture or rules and could only look at it from his solely human outlook. So he needed to understand or he and

Canin would end at odds with each other. "You said you don't know your origins. What do you know about your history? Phuro spoke and you understood Romani."

"We know our ancestors came from Romania and Hungary, traveling with the Roma. Each family unit has their own personal history."

"So you do have mates?"

"Mates being the operative word. A Ruv may have more than one mate or just a one night stand. I told you we are mostly solitary creatures except for our companion. Though we resemble wolves in our other form we are not naturally group animals. But there are those that crave family/pack or a lone Ruv who wants littles. Thus family units happen but they are not the norm. Females do usually have at least one little so we continue on. I don't want a mate," he added at Hanlan's raised eyebrow.

Hanlan contemplated that. He wouldn't lose Canin's friendship to or over a female as he was not interested in that kind of relationship either. His ex-wife had seen to that with her behavior. He would never trust another woman with his heart again. She had been the reason he's moved here after the divorce ten years ago and started anew. One worry down. "Explain to me about your culture, your rules, your morals."

"It's hard to explain in human terms."

"Try. I need to understand."

"We have basic rules as a race, but our morals are our own. As to our culture, that was lost with our origins. There are some things that are passed on through generations, but our culture as a whole is lost. Though there are legends."

"So you do have basic rules that all the Ruv follow?"

"Yes. I suppose you could call them our Ten Commandments, though each have subcategories."

"I'm guessing that Thou Shalt Not Kill isn't one of those Commandments."

"Murder is wrong, but not killing per se. Depends upon the reason, much like your laws. Wanton killing makes one Shilmulo and a threat to the rest of the Ruv. Thus the enforcers."

"Enforcers. You said you were one."

"Yes." Canin dropped his eyes to the coffee table. "The leader or Alpha of a Pack has need of policing his own as well as the Ruv as a whole. It's the size of the Pack and territory that determines the number of enforcers in the area."

Is that why you're a cop? Because you were an enforcer?"

"No." Canin shook his head. "A lot of enforcers are on the wrong size of human law. My personal morals led me down this path."

"What happened?"

"What do you mean?" Canin raised his eyes to look at Hanlan.

"Something happened that caused you to follow this path and leave the enforcer route behind." Hanlan could feel the guilt and remorse that touched Canin when he thought about being an enforcer.

"My pack died because of me being an enforcer."

"What happened?" Hanlan asked again, his voice soft.

"The Shilmulo I was after was insane. She--she burned them alive." He paused and Hanlan could feel him force his feelings down. "I told the Alpha I needed a break. So he made a deal with Phuro and here I am."

"Your jacket says you were in Vice for a year."

"Only opening when I transferred in. And truthfully I was grateful. I was a mess."

"The taking of lives doesn't seem to upset Lowell or Lupo."

"Killing's in our nature. But each Ruv has their own moral code which they follow besides the universal laws that we are all taught. Enforcers are the police of the Ruv and their moral code is in their very bones."

Hanlan noticed how he divorced himself from his words but he didn't comment on that. "You mentioned legends earlier. Tell me the one about this book that can allow one to rule the world."

"I figured you'd want to know our universal laws." Canin raised an eyebrow.

"We'll get to those. This book seems to be essential to our case."

Canin took a long swallow of beer, then settled more comfortably in his chair. "The legend goes that the Oru family unit was entrusted with the Lexicon Codex to serve the Ruv as Oracles. But a Shilmulo desired the book to rule over the World and the Oru had to hide the book. There was a fight and the Oru was killed. Before he died he had told his oldest son that 'the inscription holds the clue'. The book has many tales itself. No one knows for sure what it really is."

"Phuro said that it's not a legend. He must know something if he can state that."

Before Canin could say anything in reply, his cell phone rang and he answered with "Canin." There was a pause, then he straightened in the chair and set the beer down. Hanlan could feel his alertness and apprehension. "Thanks for the information," he said before closing the phone and returning it to his pocket. "That was Phuro. Lowell and Lupo have both disappeared."

Fear flashed through Hanlan, but he couldn't let it rule him. He set his beer on the coffee table, then stood. "Come on. Let's go."

Canin stood and put his hand on Hanlan's chest to stop him. "Go where?"

"Raven Manor. That's where they're headed." It was obvious to him. Both were obsessed with the secrets Raven Manor held. The Game was up so they would want one more chance at finding the secret to the book's whereabouts.

"Phuro can send his enforcers."

"They don't know the passageway. We're wasting time." He was sure they were already there. Fear flared again but he pushed it down again.

"I can almost smell your fear," Canin told him. "Your heart is beating fast with it."

"Catching bad guys is more than my job. It's in my blood. I know you understand that."

"Alright." Canin withdrew his hand. "But I'm calling Phuro on the way."

"Do what you gotta do." Hanlan pushed past him and headed toward the back door. "What kills your kind anyway?"

Canin didn't answer as he followed Hanlan out the door.

CHAPTER 21

No light showed nor was there a car in the drive when the detectives arrived at Raven Manor. They retrieved the flashlights they had used before, then got out of the car. The outside lights had not come on, but the glow of the full moon gave them enough light to make it to the front door. It was open an inch. The lock showed forced entry and a crowbar lying nearby told the how.

"Would my thirty-eight do anything but annoy them?" Hanlan asked Canin.

"Only if you sever the spine or hit the heart."

"That's what I thought." Hanlan pushed the door open and snapped on the flashlight. He stepped inside and hit the lights but nothing happened.

Another thought confirmed.

They left the door open and headed for the dining room, Canin snapping on his own flashlight. Neither drew their weapons. The Manor was deathly silent, the carpeted hallway muffling their own footsteps. When they made the dining room, Hanlan and Canin shown their lights on the passageway's door. It hung half open, part of it shredded.

Hanlan forced it the rest of the way open and stepped inside. A shiver of fear went down his spine, but he turned right and headed down the passageway with Canin just behind him. Nothing was waiting for them in the darkness as they continued toward the underground crypt. But Hanlan wasn't reassured. He knew what they would no doubt find there.

The detectives made it to the stairway and paused. Flickering light lit the stair and ceiling above and they could hear voices below. Someone had lit the torches on the crypt's walls and were moving about the chamber by the sound of it. Both detectives turned off and pocketed their flashlights. Canin stepped on the stairway first and led the way down.

Lupo and Lowell were circling each other on the other side of the statue. Both were in human form but fangs and claws were out. They didn't pause in their dance with each other as the detectives appeared and continued to trade swipes and growls.

Lowell grabbed one of the torches as she whirled by and tossed it from one clawed hand to the other, keeping Lupo away. Lupo lunged and then jumped away depending on Lowell's movement of the torch. They continued this as the detectives stepped off the stairway.

The two women were moving further away from the altar in their deadly dance which suited Hanlan fine. He tugged Canin toward the statue. As he had remembered there was an inscription on the altar. "What does that say?"

"It's an old saying like Phuro said."

"What does it say?" he hissed in frustration and urgency.

" 'I welcome you with outstretched arms and all the secrets within'."

Hanlan stared at the statue for a minute, then climbed onto the altar. He knelt in front of the hands and carefully lifted the stone scroll free of them.

The hands crumbled and the statue was suddenly pitted with age as if it had been weathered. Light flared around the scroll which shimmered and reshaped into a leather-bound tome.

"I didn't expect that." Hanlan's hushed voice was loud in the sudden silence.

"You will give that to me," came Lowell's voice.

Amusement seem to radiate from the book and Hanlan felt a tingle in his hands as if they had gone to sleep and the blood was now re-flowing through them. He held the book against his chest and moved so he was sitting on the altar with his feet touching the floor. Lupo was laying on the floor unmoving with Lowell standing over her, but Hanlan didn't think she was unconscious, merely playing possum. "I think not," he told Lowell.

"Then I will take it and drain you like I did that lawyer."

"So it was you who murdered Shaw." Hanlan narrowed his eyes at her. "You dressed like Lupo on purpose. You wanted her blamed for his death."

"She did kill the Graves after all. I was hoping it would keep her out of my business."

Lupo chose that moment to act. There was a shimmer and she was sinking her fangs into Lowell's thigh. Lowell screamed and shoved the torch into the wolf's face. The smell of burning hair filled the room as the wolf jerked away, taking a bit of flesh with her.

Canin froze and Hanlan could feel his fear and grief. He knew his partner was reliving his pack's death. "Fofo!" Hanlan yelled at Lowell, causing her to glance at him. As soon as her eyes were on him, he threw the book at her. It was surprisingly light and sailed straight for her.

Lowell dropped the torch and reached out to catch the book. The second she touched it she began to howl and shimmer, the book falling to the floor as she began to burn. She continued to shimmer as her skin and flesh melted away from her bones. As soon as her flesh was expended, her bones began to incinerate, turning to ash within seconds. The ash itself flared and then was gone. Nothing remained but a dark spot on the stone floor.

There were gasps from the stairway and Hanlan looked that way. Phuro and two huge men in coveralls stood just before the stairs. When he looked back, Lupo had disappeared as well, but Hanlan figured she had left via a secret exit. He ignored the new comers and moved to stand in front of his partner. "Canin."

"Hanlan," Phuro began.

"I'll deal with you in a minute," Hanlan told him, keeping his eyes on his partner. He laid his hand on Canin's chest. "Canin!"

Cognac eyes focused on him as Canin wrapped his fingers around Hanlan's wrist of the hand on his chest. "Vitsa."

"You back with us now?" Hanlan asked him. He could almost feel Canin push the memories back.

"Yes." Canin dropped his hand.

"Good." He turned toward the other three Ruv. "Were you just going to stand there while they killed each other?"

"We can't interfere with a challenge."

There was a hint of something in Phuro's voice but Hanlan wasn't in the mood to decipher what it was. "And if she attacked us?"

Phuro's silence told Hanlan all he needed to know.

Hanlan turned on his heel and stalked to the book, anger in every movement. Bending, he picked up the huge book easily and held it against his chest. He straightened and, turning, headed back to the altar. Once there he laid the book on its surface, then stepped away. "So this is what all this was about."

"Yes." The female voice came from the far corner. A cloaked figure materialized out of the shadows there and stepped forward until it was well in the flickering light of the torches. Gloved hands reached up and lowered the hood of the cloak, revealing the face of the figure.

"Mrs. Carson, what a surprise," Hanlan said as he turned to fully face her. The four Ruv just stared and Hanlan could feel Canin's shock.

"Your discovery is most unfortunate."

Hanlan raised an eyebrow.

"The Balance has been kept with the Codex's absence. If it was allowed to be studied by either side that would not be so. Too many advantages would be gained."

"You're not just the director of the AHST, are you?"

"Not in the way you mean." She smiled in amusement. "The Trust was actually founded to keep an eye on Raven Manor in case someone took the Lexicon Codex legend seriously."

"How do you even know about it?" Phuro asked, speaking up. "You are not Ruv."

"Your beloved Chosen Roma were not the only ones who knew of your kind."

Hanlan could hear the contempt in her voice. But who was it for, the Roma or the Ruv? "Now that the Codex is found what do you plan to do?"

"You'll be the unfortunate victim of the curse of this place like the Duncans and Mercer."

Canin moved closer to Hanlan in a protective stance.

"Your group was responsible for their deaths?"

"They threatened the balance like you." She made a gesture and a ball of golden light struck Canin. Her eyes widened when Canin just stood there and she threw another ball of light. That one Canin caught and fear entered her eyes as it hovered above his palm.

"You have learned the trick of energy manipulation I see," Canin said almost conversationally. "Which tells me you are older than you look. However your education in this matter is sadly lacking or you would know better than to use it on me."

"What are you talking about?" Hanlan asked. "What is that ball of light?"

"All living things give off energy," Canin explained as he kept his eyes on Carson. "In humans it's referred to as your Aura. We call it something different, but it is what we manipulate to change our form. It can also be manipulated in other ways."

"But it takes time and focus to learn those other ways," Phuro said as he eyed Carson. "And there are limitations."

Hanlan also eyed Carson. Fear shone in her eyes but she was defiant and something else glittered in her eyes. "I don't think she came alone," he said suddenly.

A shimmer and one of the other Ruv bound up the stairs in wolf form.

"Magic may not work on you but we have something that does." She pulled out a pistol from her cloak and fired two shots toward the two Ruv by the stairs.

Canin shimmered and leaped, knocking Carson to the floor. He grabbed the wrist of the gun hand with his fangs as he collapsed on top of her to keep her down. He obviously weighed more as a wolf or his weight was more in his torso than when he was human because Carson grunted and was struggling to breathe.

Hanlan snatched the pistol and tossed it away, then pulled out his handcuffs. He cuffed one hand, then motioned Canin off before flipping Carson onto her stomach and securing both hands behind her back. Once he was sure she was safely bound, he straightened and looked over at the other two Ruv.

Phuro was kneeling over his enforcer, holding a small bullet-sized dart in his one hand. He smelled it and grimaced, then tossed it away from him.

"Is he alright?" Hanlan asked.

"He will be." Phuro stood. "We are impervious to most tranquilizers and poisons. This stuff just knocks us out for a few hours." He glanced up the stairs, then looked over at Carson.

Hanlan glanced down at Carson, then looked at Phuro. There was nothing he could really do with Carson. Technically, they were all trespassing on Trust property and she had the right to defend herself. However, he knew it was certain death for her if she went with Phuro. His sense of human justice was struggling with Ruv justice. Canin leaned against his leg and Hanlan felt comfort radiating from him.

A howl echoed down the stairs, then was abruptly cut off and Phuro growled.

"You may have gotten me but you'll not leave this place with the book." Carson started laughing.

Phuro pulled out his cell phone and texted someone before putting it back. He dragged his unconscious enforcer to in front of the altar and stood there, staring at the book.

Carson had stopped laughing and had twisted around so she could stare toward the altar. "So innocent looking to be the cause of so much strife, isn't it?"

The Ruv alpha didn't answer, just continued to stare at the book.

Hanlan retrieved her pistol and walked over to the altar. He laid it beside the book and stood so he had a view of the stairs. "How long?"

Canin stood guard over Carson, though part of his attention was on the stairs as well.

"Thirty minutes."

A lot could happen in that time Hanlan knew. He went over and examined the corner Carson came from. They didn't need someone else coming up behind them and maybe they could use it if there was an exit there. No such luck. Search as he might he couldn't find a doorway of any kind. He gave up and went back to the altar.

Canin growled and a small object rolled down the stairs, smoke issuing from it.

The assault had begun.

CHAPTER 22

Ablack-clad man had followed the smoke grenade and was met by Phuro the brown wolf. Out came the throat and the blood went down Phuro's. Now Hanlan knew what had become of the blood from the Graves and Shaw.

Phuro retreated, leaving the body at the foot of the stairs.

The smoke strangely stopped at the altar and didn't get any thicker. It lightly blanketed the stairway, but it was thin enough that they could see if anyone came down.

Suddenly there were screams and shots echoing from above. After a few minutes, they were abruptly cut off and silence reigned again.

Phuro returned to human form but remained by

the altar, his eyes never leaving the stairway.

Lupo came down the stairs and stopped on the bottom step. She and Phuro stared at each other for a long moment, then she looked at Hanlan. "I do not think myself Shilmulo. This place and its legacy are mine. I will do what I have to to reclaim it." She turned and with a shimmer bounded up the stairs in wolf form.

"You're not going to detain her?"

"For what?" Phuro asked, his eyes still on the stairs. "She was defending her claim."

Hanlan could sense he would get nowhere if he persisted so he let it lie for now. "You think she got them all?" Harlan asked, looking up the stairs as far as he could from where he was standing.

"We'll just wait here until my other enforcers arrive," Phuro told him before turning to look down at Carson. "What do you have to say for yourself, gorger?"

Carson just glared at him.

"No excuses for your actions?"

"I did what I had to do to maintain the balance."

Phuro grunted and went over to Carson, reaching down to pull her to her feet.

Once she was standing, Hanlan moved to stand in front of them both. "What are you planning to do with her?"

"She will pay for her crimes."

The hard look in Phuro's eyes told Hanlan how she would pay. "What's the difference between what she did and what Lupo did? They both acted on their convictions."

"You surely don't want me to let her go?"

"No, she should pay. But Lupo did worse and you let her walk." Hanlan wanted understanding. He needed to see justice done, not vengeance or revenge. And his human viewpoint wasn't seeing that. One shouldn't go free and another punished for virtually the same crime.

Phuro's eyes softened as a flicker of understanding appeared across his face. "You are thinking like a human, not a Ruv, which is understandable. Carson did not do these things for honorable reasons. Hers were hate crimes if you want to put it in human terms."

"I don't understand."

"When she said our chosen weren't the only ones who knew about us, I realized she was quite right and who created the Trust. There is a group of humans that despise the Roma and the Ruv and hunt us both."

"You both are threats to the balance," Carson said.

"What's this balance you keep mentioning?" Hanlan asked her.

"The Ruv are arrogant and believe they should rule the world with humans as their slaves and there are some arrogant humans that believe they themselves should rule with both Ruv and other humans as their slaves. We are tasked with keeping either from happening."

"Keeping my kind ignorant of our history and culture helps that how?" Phuro asked with barely concealed contempt.

"You Ruv would rise up and takeover."

"Demand equal rights perhaps but like humans

not all of us are megalomaniacs. Your group wants to keep us ignorant so we are easily controlled." He turned his eyes toward the stairway. "Good of you to join us, gentlemen."

Hanlan turned toward the stairs.

Two Ruv stood there in black coveralls. One was blond, the other dark-haired but both were slender with muscles straining the material of their garments.

"Where are the others?" Phuro asked them as he escorted Carson toward the other Ruv.

"Recon," the blond replied.

"I doubt she left anyone alive before she went." Phuro stopped in front of the two Ruv and shoved Carson at the blond. "She's a leader of the Hunters."

The blond grabbed her arm and turning marched her up the stairs.

"I need guards 24/7 for this chamber. No one in or out until I say so."

"What about the torches?"

"Replace them with battery-powered lights." Phuro turned on his heel and headed back to the altar while the other Ruv went up the stairs.

Canin had returned to his human form and was standing next to Hanlan by the altar. Hanlan had opened the book and both of them were now staring at the symbols on the pages.

"This doesn't look like the inscription letters," Hanlan commented.

"It's our native language. When we joined with the Roma we adopted their language as the common tongue." Phuro slipped on the glasses hanging from his neck and looked at the book. "I have a basic understanding of our language. We will have to get one of our scholars who specializes in our language."

"I'm not going to be a glorified page-turner," Hanlan told him. "You need to find an Oru, one that it will accept."

"What do you mean, one that it will accept?"

Hanlan went over the impressions he had received from the book, then said, "It's keyed to Oru blood, but it has a presence, an essence."

"It's alive?"

"Sort of. I can't explain what I don't understand."

"You have Oru blood?" Canin spoke up.

"No." Hanlan closed the book and turned away from the altar. "Looks like you're going to have to do a bit more creative writing," he told Canin. "'Cause I don't know how to explain all this."

"We'll take care of the bodies and clean-up," Phuro told him. "But none of this can be put in a report."

"I know." Canin nodded. "I'll think of something by tomorrow morning."

"I'd like to go home now," Hanlan said. He was tired, in more ways than one. He wanted to go back to his apartment and not think about anything.

"I'll talk to you tomorrow evening." Phuro stepped out of his way.

Hanlan nodded and both detectives headed for the stairway. Canin fell into step behind Hanlan and followed him up the stairs. They retrieved their flashlights from their pockets and went into the passageway, following it to the shredded dining room exit. The lights had been restored and the dining room was lit up when they entered from the passageway. Both detectives flipped their lights off and slipped the flashlights into their pockets as they headed toward the foyer.

An enforcer passed them in the hallway, but neither they nor the enforcer acknowledged each other as they continued on their separate ways.

Two vans and a sports car were parked behind Hanlan's car in the circular drive. He noticed that the outside lights were not on. Phuro's enforcers must have shut them off some how to keep the neighbor's from seeing more than shadows even with the full moon.

Canin got in the passenger side while Hanlan slid into the driver's seat. Neither spoke as Hanlan drove away from Raven Manor nor did either of them look back. They had both had enough of the place. However they both knew they would have to return again in the not too distant future.

"You want me to drop you off at the station?" Hanlan asked after a while.

"I'm not leaving you alone."

Hanlan just nodded. He had figured that, what with the protective vibes coming off Canin, and so was heading toward his apartment. But he hadn't wanted to assume. When he got to his apartment he pulled into his slot and both of them got out of the car. Hanlan led the way to his door, then into his kitchen. He got himself a shot glass, then raised an eyebrow at Canin.

When Canin nodded, Hanlan pulled down another shot glass, then poured them both some whiskey. He returned the bottle to its place, then handed Canin a glass before throwing back his own shot. Leaving his glass on the counter, Hanlan headed into the living room and stood, waiting.

Canin threw back his own shot, then followed Hanlan into the living room.

"You can take the other bedroom," Hanlan told him.

"I'll be fine out here."

Hanlan looked at him. He could tell Canin had no notion of sleeping tonight.

There was a shimmer and Canin hopped up on the couch in wolf form.

"Have it your way then." Hanlan shook his head and headed into the bedroom. Sleep was calling, though he didn't think it would be a restful night. The wolves would no doubt be back.

CHAPTER 23

The wolves had been suspiciously absent from his dreams and Hanlan had gotten actual sleep. He hurried through his morning routine and dressed in an older suit before stepping out into the living room.

Canin was sprawled on the couch, sound asleep.

Hanlan went into the kitchen and grabbed two breakfast burritos from the freezer and popped them in the microwave. He then made two cups of instant coffee since he had not set the coffee maker up last night nor did he feel like doing it this morning. Memories stirred but he pushed them away and concentrated on the now.

Canin wandered in in a new suit.

"How do you do that?" Hanlan asked him as he

handed Canin a burrito and coffee before consuming his own.

"Energy and matter manipulation," Canin told him between bites and sips.

"And your phone and things?"

"Energy pockets."

Hanlan grunted and finished his breakfast. He rinsed his cup out, then set it in the strainer before heading toward the door. "Let's go. You can tell me the story for this case on the way."

"It all depends on whether the report on the shoes is in. If it is, everything goes onto Lowell," Canin said as he put his cup in the sink before following Hanlan out the door. "She was obsessed with Raven Manor."

"True enough." Hanlan slid into the driver's seat as Canin got into the passenger side. "Or obsessed with the Curse?"

"That will work." Canin nodded.

They made good time to the station and hurried up to the bullpen. The report was indeed in Hanlan's in-box and both detectives settled at their desks as Hanlan pulled out the report to read.

"Shoe print matched with one of Lowell's. They said it had been cleaned but they found one speck of blood and are running a DNA test."

"Excellent." Canin slid up to his computer and started typing. "I'm not putting in our little trip last night in the notes. Just that we suspect she might go there, then I'll have some uniforms stop by. They can discover what's left to discover."

Hanlan nodded and put the report on his desk before standing. "I'll tell the Captain about the shoe print and she's probably have the One-Eight try and pick her up."

Canin gave him a nod, then returned his attention to his screen.

Putting on his game face, Hanlan headed to the captain's office. She was usually here before everyone else so he was surprised to find the office empty. He was about to leave when she hurried in, carrying a large latte.

"Did you need something, Detective?"

"Wanted to update you on the shoe print. There was a match with one of Professor Lowell's and the Lab found a speck of blood. It's human so they're running a DNA test now."

Gardner sat in her chair and took a sip of her drink. "Do we know if they knew each other?"

"Probably not. But he was handling the Graves' probate, specifically Raven Manor. She was obsessed with that place—though more about the supposed Curse on it."

"I'll have the One-Eight pull her in and bring her here for questioning."

"Good." Hanlan turned to go.

"You look better this morning, Detective."

"I managed to actually sleep last night."

"Good. You needed it."

"Thank you, Captain, for your words of praise," Hanlan told her before heading back to his desk. He sat down and leaned back in his chair with a sigh.

"She going to talk to the One-Eight?" Canin asked as he hung up the desk phone and looked at Hanlan.

"Yeah."

"I just sent some uniforms to check out the Manor," Canin told him.

"I doubt they fixed the passageway door in the dining room. So hopefully, Phuro's guards can stay out of sight."

"With Phuro one can never tell. We still going to the funeral this afternoon?"

"Yes, we need to tell Shaw that we have a suspect in his father's murder."

Both of them were speaking in a low voice to insure others would have a hard time hearing them a midst the normal noises of the bullpen.

Hanlan leaned forward and started gathering up the reports for the case. He stacked them in a pile, then opened one of his big drawers. Grimacing at the mess inside, he reached in and pulled out some cardboard. He manipulated the cardboard into a box and lid which he set on the open drawer before filing the reports in the box.

Canin handed him the autopsy reports he had on his desk and Hanlan filed them in the box. He watched Hanlan open his middle drawer and immediately shoved it shut. "They haven't found who ransacked your desk yet, did they?"

"They haven't called me about it anyway." He looked over at Canin. "You got a marker?"

Opening his middle drawer, Canin reached in and pulled out a black marker. He tossed it to Hanlan before closing his drawer. "Keep it. I have another one."

Hanlan caught the marker and leaned over the box to write on the front space. He wrote quickly and then put the marker in his middle drawer.

"Anticipating a confession, Detective?" the captain asked as she came up to his desk. "If you are you'll have to wait. The One-Eight reported that it looks like Professor Lowell has 'flown the coup'. She was not at the University or her home. No one has had contact with her since the serving of the warrant yesterday."

"That's interesting," Hanlan commented.

"I thought so too." The captain paused. "I'm going home as usual at noon, but call me if you need anything or something comes up."

Hanlan nodded and the captain headed back to her office. He turned to look at Canin but before he could say anything, Canin's desk phone rang.

"Canin," the Ruv said into it when he picked it up. There was a pause, then he said, "Alright. Thanks for the call." before hanging up. "The uniforms didn't see anything suspicious, no signs of forced entry or open windows. They said it was locked up tight."

"Add that to the notes to cover the uniforms."

Nodding, Canin rolled up to his computer and typed for a while as Hanlan went back to organizing the reports in the box. Both sat back when they finished and looked at each other. They both honestly didn't know what to do right then.

Hanlan's desk phone rang and he answered with "Hanlan." There was a pause, then he rubbed his hand over his face. "Sorry, Jack. I forgot all about that. This case has been keeping me busy." Another pause. "Yeah, we did found them all. I can tell you over a beer tonight if you're up for it." A longer pause. "Okay. Six-thirty at the bar. See you then, Jack," he said before before hanging up the phone. He rubbed his face again, then looked at Canin.

Canin raised an eyebrow.

"I was supposed to meet Reach at the bar this morning. To talk about the past happenings at Raven Manor."

"By 'the bar' you mean The Old Haunt on Jameson?"

"Yes, most of us just refer to it as 'the bar'."

"Vice preferred O'Reilly's on Fifth. I didn't care for it much."

Both detectives stop talking as they saw Howell and Deneque headed their way.

"We heard you had a break in the Shaw murder." Howell spoke as usual as he and Deneque crowded around Hanlan's desk. "That one of the shoes matched."

"Yep. But she did a runner," Hanlan told them.

"Well, she knew the game was up when we came for the shoes."

Hanlan nodded in agreement.

"You said the funeral for Shaw is this afternoon."

"Yeah, Canin and I are going. We need to update the son."

"If you need anything, call us."

Hanlan nodded again and watched as the other two detectives went back to their own desks. "They're bored. They must still be off rotation."

"As long as they don't poke too deep into this case."

Before Hanlan could say anything, his phone

rang and he answered with his usual "Hanlan." He listened for a moment, then said, "Call CSU and have them tow it to the lot. Thanks for the call." He hung up and looked at Canin. "They found Lowell's car on the side of the road near the University."

"Ah. Phuro is thorough."

"I got to talk to the captain about getting a warrant to search it." Hanlan stood and headed to the captain's office. He stopped in the doorway and knocked on the frame. "Captain."

"Detective."

"We need a warrant to search Professor Lowell's car. It was found abandoned near the University."

"I'll get it sent directly to CSU." The captain picked up her phone, then paused as Hanlan hadn't moved. "Something else, Detective?"

"Canin and I are going to Shaw's funeral this afternoon. We're going to have a long lunch and take off afterwards."

"Okay. See you Monday then."

Hanlan nodded and, turning, headed back to his desk. Once there he put the lid on the box and slid his chair under his desk. "Let's go."

Canin raised an eyebrow.

"We're going back to my place. I'll order a pizza for lunch but we need to talk."

"I thought you didn't want to."

"I don't. But we need to."

Canin nodded and stood. He slid his own chair under his desk and turned to follow Hanlan.

Both detectives left the bullpen and headed to the elevator. They rode down in silence. Sgt. Dan wasn't at the window so they made the back doors without incident or disturbance. They hurried down the stairs and into the car as the wind had picked up and was a bit nippy. Fall was showing itself more and more.

Hanlan kept his mind off the events of last night as he drove. He didn't want to be overwhelmed while operating the vehicle. Once at his apartment, he would let go. He was good at compartmentalizing but he wanted this out.

The detectives got out and headed into the apartment as soon as Hanlan had parked in his slot. Hanlan pulled two beers out of the refrigerator before they both went into the living room. He handed one to Canin, then sat on the couch, letting Canin take the chair again. Popping the top off, he took a long swig of the beer.

"I can feel the turmoil," Canin said.

"I watched a scroll turn into a book, a person burn to death in a magical fire, and another walk away without consequences though I know she committed murder. Then there's Ms. Carson. I think I'm entitled to feel conflicted, maybe even have a breakdown."

Canin set his beer on the coffee table and shimmering transformed into his wolf form. He climbed up on the couch and laid his head on Hanlan's lap.

Hanlan shifted to accommodate Canin's large form and began petting his head. He could feel comfort radiating from Canin and unconsciously relaxed. "This doesn't solve anything, you know?"

The comfort ratcheted up a notch.

Hanlan took another swig, then dropped his head

back to the couch back. It was a bit awkward but he didn't care. He just blanked his mind and petted Canin, wallowing in the comfort being offered.

CHAPTER 24

Both of the detectives had fallen asleep and when they awoke, they barely had time to grab a breakfast burrito from Hanlan's freezer before they had to leave to make the funeral.

Hanlan drove under and through the large metal gate of Harlin Cemetery, following the winding road until he came upon the cars of the participants of the funeral. He pulled in behind the last car and parked.

The detectives got out and headed toward the tent they could see among-st the tombstones. Some people were seated, others were standing around the tent. A casket sat in the middle of the tent over an open grave and a priest stood next to it by a small easel with a photo of the deceased. A wreathe of flowers lay on top of casket and that was the only décor.

Stephen Shaw saw them and came over to them as they stopped at one corner of the tent. "Detectives. Anything new?"

"We have a suspect. But she's disappeared." Hanlan got straight to the point.

"She?" Shaw gave Hanlan a calculating look. "Professor Lowell?"

"We can't give you specifics as the investigation is still ongoing, but, if I may ask, did he know her?"

"Not that I know of." Shaw shook his head. "I think I was the only one at the firm who had that distinct dishonor."

The priest cleared his throat just then, and said, "It's time."

Everyone but the detectives gathered around the coffin as Shaw left them to join the priest. The detectives remained at the corner and watched the mourners as the priest opened his bible and took out a card.

"Robert didn't want me to preach and talk about how good he was or read passages over him," the priest said. "He gave me a little note he wanted me to read. Of course he thought he would died of his cancer. He said it was written by his wife before she died of cancer and told all he believed needed to be said. "

Stephen Shaw dropped his head as the priest cleared his throat again before starting.

"I don't want you to mourn for me. I've lived my life and now it's time to say goodbye. You still have things to do here and you need to get on with doing them. I'll always be in your heart and I'll never be far from you. A beloved memory to keep you warm in this cold world." He slipped the card back in the bible and closed it. "May they both rest in peace together."

Everyone was silent for a moment after the priest finished, then Stephen Shaw raised his head and stepped closer to the casket. "Goodbye, Father." His voice was thick with emotion. He laid his hand on the casket for a second, then turned to the priest and shook his hand. "Thank you, Father Callahan."

The others came over to Stephen Shaw to shake his hand and offer condolences before leaving. Soon only Shaw, the detectives, and the two gravediggers were left. Shaw and the detectives walked together toward the cars while the gravediggers began to finish their work.

Canin's cell phone rang and he pulled it out to glance at it. He stopped and turned to answer it, motioning Hanlan on.

Hanlan and Shaw continued on to the road and stopped by Shaw's gray BMW. Shaw pulled out his keys and bounced them in his hand, then looked at Hanlan. "I know I can't know the details but can you at least tell me why?"

"You saw how she was at the Graves' funeral."

"Raven Manor." Shaw stood there a second with a bowed head, then turned and opened his car door. "Keep me in the loop as much as you can, detective." He slid into his car and closed the door. Seconds later, he drove away.

Hanlan turned and headed for his own car. Canin was waiting for him there and Hanlan raised an eyebrow at him.

"That was Phuro. He's going to meet us at your place. He has some information you may want to hear."

They both got into the car, then Hanlan carefully drove out of the cemetery and headed toward his apartment. Neither spoke during the drive.

Hanlan pulled into his slot when he arrived at his apartment and both detectives got out of the car. They headed toward the door, then paused as they saw Phuro.

"Detectives." Phuro straightened from where he was leaning against the house. He joined them and they continued on to the entrance.

Once he had the door open, Hanlan motioned them in, then followed them and closed the door behind himself. "Want a beer?" he asked as he went to the refrigerator. Phuro declined, but Canin nodded so Hanlan grabbed two beers before leading the way into the living room. He handed a beer to Canin, then sat on the couch while the two Ruv took the chairs. "Alright, let's hear it," he said as he opened his beer before he took a twig.

"Carson had one of her cop lackeys break into your desk looking for the files on the past murders." Phuro got straight into it. "She was afraid you might find something as she heard you were a good detective. Probably from the same lackey."

"There's one of her Trust people at the precinct?"

"More than one from what little I could get from her about her Hunters. She was forthcoming with what she did, but clammed up about her people. But I thought you both should be warned."

Hanlan took another swig, then asked, "Did she tell you about the past murders?"

"She was eager to speak her excuses for them as if it was a source of pride."

Sighing, Hanlan swirled the beer in the bottle, then looked Phuro in the eye. "Is she dead?"

"Yes." Phuro met his eyes squarely.

Hanlan stared into the cognac eyes for a moment, then dropped his eyes and took another swig of beer. At least there was closure, though not the way Hanlan would have pursued it as this way there was no chance for redemption. Of course some were beyond redemption but most should be at least given the chance. He took a longer swig of beer before looking up. "Anything else?"

"Yes." Phuro leaned forward, his eyes intent. "The book."

Hanlan just stared at him silently.

After a few minutes of silence, Phuro sighed and leaned back. "Several lines have some Oru blood but none with substantial percentages."

"Ms. Lupo?" Hanlan asked.

"Her line is one with a higher percentage."

"Hmm." Hanlan took another swig of beer. "I got a question for you."

Phuro raised an eyebrow.

"What's going to happen with the Trust? They own Raven Manor and if most of them are these Hunters..." he trailed off.

"We cleaned up everything except the passageway door. No one's come around from the Trust, but we don't think that's going to hold much longer. So if you would be amendable, I would like to move the book to a safer place."

"Now?"

"Yes."

Hanlan drank the rest of his beer and set the bottle down on the coffee table before standing. "Okay."

Canin had been silently drinking his own beer as the other two talked. Now he set his own half-empty bottle on the coffee table next to Hanlan's and stood as well.

Phuro got up from the chair and led the way to the back door with Hanlan and Canin behind him. The three of them exited the apartment and made their way to the car. They got in with Phuro taking the back seat and Hanlan backed out of his slot before heading toward Raven Manor. None of them spoke during the drive.

The circular drive was empty so Hanlan pulled up right in front of the door. They all got out and went up to the front door. It was locked and Hanlan was surprised that his key still worked, but didn't comment as he opened the door. The three of them entered and Hanlan closed the door behind them before they headed for the dining room. A shredded door greeted them there but they entered and went down the passageway to the crypt stairway. Phuro led the way down, the other two following.

A black Ruv wolf got up from in front of the altar as they entered the crypt. Though similar in color to Canin's wolf form Hanlan could tell it was different from Canin.

"You are relieved," Phuro told the wolf. "Return to your regular duties."

The wolf dipped its head, then bounded up the stairs and was gone.

Hanlan walked over to the altar and picked up the book, his hands tingling again. He held it against his chest and turned toward the stairway.

Phuro led the way up with Hanlan behind him and Canin bringing up the rear. They returned to the dining room, then headed to the foyer. Hanlan handed Canin the key so he could lock the door behind them, then they left the Manor. Canin opened the trunk for Hanlan who laid the book inside before closing said trunk. The three of them had just taken a step back when a van came through the gate and pulled up behind them.

The logo on the side of the van was for the Alsena Historical Society and Trust.

CHAPTER 25

Three men in black plus a woman in a suit got out of the van and came up to the three by the car. The three men stood in a half circle behind the woman and watched with cold eyes. Hanlan did not like them at all and the woman wasn't giving off warm vibes either.

"Good, you're here," he said before the woman could speak. "The professor told us someone was seen picking the lock. When we got here the door was locked, but we went inside anyway. We found the passageway door shredded, but didn't check anything out because the professor wanted to call your director to see what she wanted done. However with you here maybe you can give us permission to search the premises for intruders."

"I take it you're Detectives Hanlan and Canin?" the woman asked.

"Yes. I called the professor to tell him we were going to release the place and he could pick up the key anytime but he told me someone was trespassing. We figured it might be our suspect so we picked the professor up and came here."

"I'm Assistant Director Jennifer Cowen." the woman said. "How do you know Professor Ulven?"

"He was referred to us when we asked for information about the Manor," Hanlan told her.

Phuro nodded and nervously cleaned his glasses, acting the shy and nervous professor to a T.

"Ah." Cowen watched Phuro clean his glasses for a minute, then said, "You were right to have them wait." She turned her eyes to Hanlan and held out her hand. "I'll take the key. My colleagues and I will search the place."

"Professor Lowell is dangerous. She's already killed at least one person because of her obsession with this place."

"We'll be careful." She kept her hand out.

At Hanlan's nod, Canin stepped forward and laid the key in her hand. He then moved back to Hanlan's side, his eyes watching the three men behind Cowen.

"Thank you for your diligence. But we can take it from here," Cowen said as she closed her hand around the key.

"Do you need my help?" Phuro asked in a timid voice.

"No." Her voice was bland but her eyes were cold.

"Then I'll ride back with the detectives."

"That will be fine." She seem to dismiss them all as she turned and headed for the front door with the men following behind her.

Phuro and the two detectives moved casually to get into the car and Hanlan drove cautiously away. Once he was far enough away, he pulled over and looked back at Phuro. "That was too close."

"Yes."

"So where to?"

"You know where the Carnegie branch of the library is?"

Hanlan nodded and turned back around before getting back on the road. "You think Cowen will be the new director?" he asked as he drove.

"There are two Assistant Directors. Either one can take over the duties, but I don't know which will be voted in by the Board."

"That one is cold," Hanlan told him. "She doesn't like you one bit. And she doesn't buy that timid act of yours."

"She's a Hunter through and through," Phuro agreed. "She wants us all either dead or under a collar. Bryan Deneque is more like Carson was. Believing in the hype they use to recruit some of the new people to their cause."

"Deneque?"

"Detective Deneque's father," Canin confirmed. "But they don't get along."

"Huh. So you don't think he's the Trust's mole?"

"Highly unlikely." Canin shrugged. "But you never know."

Hanlan pulled into a parking lot and glanced

back at Phuro. "Now what? I don't think you want the front door."

"No. Follow the building around to the back."

The gray stone two story building wasn't long and they had come in the side parking lot so it took but a minute for Hanlan to follow the direction. At the back there was a wrought iron fence along part of the back and that was where Phuro directed him. Hanlan parked in front of the fence and they all got out. After Hanlan retrieved the book, they rounded the fence and went down the ramp it partially enclosed.

Unlocking the door at the bottom, Phuro ushered them in and locked the door behind them. He hurried them through a second door, then paused. "This is the rare book room," he told them before moving over to an upright glass and wood case. Opening the case he gestured for Hanlan to lay the book inside.

Hanlan carefully laid the book on the velvet lining. As soon as he let go, the book flipped open and they all stepped back.

When nothing else happened, Phuro moved back and closed the case, locking it with a strange-looking lock. "This will keep it safe from human hands and most Ruv."

"Most?" Hanlan asked.

"There's a trick to the lock. If you don't know it, it won't open."

Hanlan nodded, then looked around.

The room was medium sized and had waist-high shelving with cases dotted here and there. A study area was near the other end and it was a bit cool in temperature. There was another door near the study area plus an archway on the left wall.

Hiding a book among other books was a good idea. Hanlan looked back at Phuro. "Why this library branch?"

"I come here all the time for my research, but mainly because it's staffed by several of us."

A woman came through the archway and paused before heading over to them. "I thought I heard voices. Good afternoon, Professor Ulven." Her cognac eyes looked large behind her glasses.

"Just stopped by to see the new book." His voice was bland.

"I see." She glanced at the case. "Will you be long? It's almost time for Professor Simpson to come in."

"We're leaving right now, Ms. Gayl." He gave her a nod, then ushered the detectives back the way they had come. Once they were back outside, Phuro insured that the door was locked, then led the way up the ramp.

A van was parked beside Hanlan's car.

All three of them stopped at the top of the ramp and stared at the van. It was white with no logo and Hanlan would guess no license plate. Canin and Phuro both tensed when two large men exited the van so Hanlan suspected these people were not friends or members of Phuro's Pack. The three of them watched as the men open the side door and an older man stepped out. His hair and coloring was the same as his son's but his eyes were an icy blue.

Phuro moved forward a bit. "Assistant Director Deneque. To what do I owe the pleasure?" His voice was upbeat and an eyebrow was raised. No hint of the apprehension that this meeting was no doubt causing.

"It has come to my attention that you are involved again with Raven Manor." His voice was stern and cold.

"That is our fault, Mr. Deneque," Hanlan said. It had sounded like a reprimand to Hanlan, but the tightening around Phuro's eyes said it was much more.

Deneque turned his attention to Hanlan.

"We were referred to him as a source of information on the Manor when we were assigned the Graves' murder," he continued.

"I see." His voice hadn't softened but his eyes held understanding.

"I couldn't turn down a request by the police," Phuro said with a bit of nervousness thrown in.

"No." Deneque looked back at Phuro. "Are you headed back to the Trust?"

"Yes." Phuro nodded.

"Then you can ride with us so you don't inconvenience the detectives."

"We were done, weren't we, Detectives?" Phuro asked, looking back over his shoulder at Hanlan and Canin.

"Yes, though we might need you to sign a statement later," Canin said before Hanlan could speak. "Thank you for your help."

Phuro nodded and moved to join the Trust members. Deneque nodded to the detectives, then the four of them moved back to the van and got in with Deneque and Phuro in the back.

"Deneque was not happy with Phuro," Hanlan commented as the van drove away.

"He knew it was a risk to go with them, but he wanted them away from here. Besides he's the Alpha for a reason. He's capable of handling them, one way or another."

"I hope so." Hanlan started toward the car with Canin following. "Let's go to the bar. We can get a burger and wait there for Reach. He might come in early."

"Sounds good."

Both detectives got into the car and drove out of the back parking lot onto the street. Hanlan took a left and headed downtown toward Jameson Street. He took a few shortcuts to cut the time down and miss the afternoon traffic. So it was less than twenty minutes later that he was heading down Jameson.

The whole of Jameson street was a line of buildings built against each other with alleyways dotted here and there where a building had been torn down. Hanlan pulled into one of the alleyways to get to the parking lot behind the bar. Trash bins decorated the plain-looking back of the buildings and Hanlan parked near the one by the bar's back entrance. It was too early or too late for the main crowd, depending on the shift. This was after all a cop bar.

Hanlan and Canin got out of the car and headed in the back entrance. They followed the long corridor to the alcove that held the restrooms, stopping there for a moment before stepping into the bar.

The bar itself stretched out beside them to the

right. Booths lined most of the outer three walls and the half two walls that divided the pool area from the rest of the bar. Small square tables with wooden chairs were spread out across the floor space except where the two pool tables were. There high stools were set around the area. A curtain was covering a doorway on the back wall that Hanlan knew led into a private dining room. The lighting was dim and smoke filled the air, even though there were No Smoking signs on the wall, but the wood and brass still gleamed.

There were three men at the bar and two guys playing pool. Four of the booths were occupied and several of the tables. During the week after the multiple shifts let out it was usually standing room only. The weekends were slower days for the bar.

Hanlan headed for a booth with Canin following. They slid in on either side and a young waitress in a black mini-dress came over to them with a large menu.

"What will you have, boys?" Her voice was perky, but her eyes were tired.

"A burger and fries for both of us, Milli," Hanlan told her. "With the daily beer."

Milli nodded and left with the menu.

"The Haunt serves good burgers and fries plus finger food but it's main draw is its liquor. Ten different beers on tap plus those fifty-two bottles on the wall behind the bar. A drinker's dream."

"Which is why I like it," Jack Reach said as he slid into the seat next to Hanlan.

"Jack, I want you to meet my new partner, Tom Canin."

"A pleasure to--," Jack trailed off as he met Canin's eyes. "Ghostwolf."

<h1 style="text-align:center">CHAPTER 26</h1>

Jack had whispered the word but both Hanlan and Canin had heard him. However before either could say or do anything in response, the waitress returned and asked Jack if he wanted anything.

"Just my usual Kentucky Bourbon, Milli," Jack said after a moment. As soon as she left, Jack dropped his eyes from Canin. "Sorry for my staring. I just ain't seen one of you for a while."

"Then you don't get out much," Hanlan said. "Because I seemed to be running into them everywhere."

Milli returned with Jack's drink and they waited for her to leave before speaking again.

"Well, I knew there were some in the City but I

don't hang out where they do." Jack took a sip of his drink and savored it for a moment before he swallowed it. "I guess you're both curious as to how I know about Ghostwolves."

Canin was staring at Jack's hands, his strangely calloused and scarred hands. "You're a Hunter."

"Was. Until I uncovered the truth."

They stopped talking as Milli came with their food. She set the plates and beer in front of Hanlan and Canin, then left again after making sure Jack didn't want anything else.

"The truth?" Hanlan asked as he picked up his burger. He and Canin started eating as Jack nodded. That breakfast burrito was long gone.

"They got this great lie about protecting the balance of the world. However they just want to keep humans on the top of the food chain by suppressing—and eventually enslaving—the Ghostwolves."

"How did you end up here in Alsena?" Hanlan asked before continuing to eat.

"I had gotten some information that this city was important to their plans so I came here and have been snooping all these years."

"That's how come you know where all the files are."

"Yep." He took another sip of the bourbon and smacked his lips after he swallowed. "This is fine bourbon."

Hanlan pushed his empty plate away and grabbed his beer. He took a sip and rinsed his mouth with it before he swallowed. "This beer isn't bad either."

Canin set his plate on top of Hanlan's and sipped his own beer. "Not bad at all," he agreed.

"What were you going to tell me about Raven Manor?" Hanlan asked Jack.

"I was going to just let you ask me questions. But I gather you know quite a bit about it now."

"Yes," was all that Hanlan said.

"I don't blame you for not trusting me. All I'll ask is if you've solved your case?"

"Yes."

There must have been something in his voice because Jack looked at him. "You don't sound happy."

"I'm not. Justice has only partially been served."

Jack glanced at the silent Canin, then returned his eyes to Hanlan. "It's hubris to think human law is the only true law."

"Murder is murder."

"All depends on the reason whether it's murder or manslaughter or self-defense."

"Definitely not self-defense."

"You humans have a saying—Karma's a bitch," Canin said, speaking up suddenly.

Hanlan looked at Canin for a minute, then took a swig of his beer. Things did indeed come around though it may take years. He nodded, then asked Jack, "Did you know Deneque's father is a Hunter?"

Jack nodded.

"Do you think he's a mole for them?"

"I doubt it. From what I hear he and the old man don't get along. Could be a ruse, of course."

"Someone broke into my desk for them."

"I'll keep an ear out." Jack threw back the rest of

the bourbon and set the glass back on the table before standing. "I got things to do now that I've seen you. I'll see you around."

Hanlan and Canin gave him a wave with their beer, then watched as he walked away. When he disappeared down the hallway, they turned back to each other. But before either of them could speak, Canin's cell phone beeped.

Canin pulled it out and called up the text message, holding up a finger for Hanlan to wait. Dropping his finger, he read the message, then texted back something before returning the phone to his pocket. "That was Phuro. He's back at the Trust, a little worse for wear but fine."

Hanlan raised an eyebrow.

"It was him," Canin said in reply to the unspoken but understood question. "Also he said his 'talk' with Deneque was enlightening. The break-in at the morgue? That was at Deneque's instigation."

"How'd he find that out? I doubt Deneque told him that."

"I don't know." Canin shrugged.

Hanlan took a swig of his beer, then set the bottle on the table. "You ready to go?"

Canin had been drinking and eating while Jack was talking too and was almost done with his beer as well. "Yeah," he answered as he set his own beer down.

Hanlan stood and pulled out his wallet. He threw a few bills on the table as Canin slid out of the booth. They both headed toward the back door and passed through the hallway. Hanlan stopped just outside the door and staggered a bit when Canin ran into him.

"What..?" Canin began before falling silent when Hanlan sidestepped so Canin could see what had made him stop.

Standing a few feet away was Sgt. Dan. In his hand was a .38 revolver and he had it pointed at Hanlan.

Canin gave a low growl and shifted his weight.

"While these bullets will only irritate you they will hurt Detective Hanlan," Sgt. Dan said as he held the weapon steadily on Hanlan. "I will be able to fire at least two rounds before you get to me."

"What do you want?" Canin growled.

Hanlan remained still where he was. He could feel the tension in Canin's body and the rage in his mind. The rage was barely held back and Hanlan didn't want to provoke it any more than Sgt. Dan already had.

"I want to know what happen to Madeline."

"Who?" Hanlan asked.

"Mrs. Carson," Canin growled.

"Ah. Why would we know what happened to her?" Hanlan raised an eyebrow at Sgt. Dan.

"You were at Raven Manor last night."

"How did you come to that conclusion?"

"Don't jerk me around," Sgt. Dan said through clenched teeth as he glared at Hanlan. "I know you were there."

"What do you want me to say?" Hanlan could almost feel the effort Canin was making to hold himself back. He needed to do something to calm things down or there would be violence.

But before he could say anything else they were

shoved from behind as another patron of the bar thrust his way past them.

Hanlan heard two retorts from the .38, then felt a warm sensation at his left shoulder before falling against the wall of the bar. Pain flared and he hissed but managed to regain his feet. Beside him on the ground was the rude patron, unconscious or dead, he didn't know. He raised his eyes and looked toward where Sgt. Dan had been standing.

Canin was in wolf form standing over the fallen form of Sgt. Dan. He dropped the gun and hand he had in his mouth and went for the throat.

Noise came from the bar. They would have heard the gunshots. "Canin!" Hanlan hissed at his partner. "Change back."

A shimmer and Canin was headed back to him in human form. He touched Hanlan's suit at the shoulder, causing Hanlan to hiss in pain. "I'm sorry. But they can't know that you're hurt."

Warmth spread through Hanlan's shoulder and it went numb. He looked down and his suit jacket was clean, no blood showing, and he raised an eyebrow.

"I'll tell you later."

Just then the bartender and two of the other patrons came out. Hanlan let Canin explain this mess and just nodded where he needed to. Even with the numbing, he was barely hanging on to consciousness. He aroused himself sufficiently to make it to the car and get in the passenger seat when they were told they could go but as soon as they hit the road he was out.

CHAPTER 27

Pain brought Hanlan to consciousness. He tried to move away, but something or someone was holding him still. He tried to open his eyes but they were too heavy, and he began to struggle.

"Don't move about," a harsh female voice said. "You'll undo my work."

Hanlan suddenly became aware of Canin's voice murmuring in his ear and stopped moving to listen.

"It's okay. Nodi's fixing your shoulder. Just lay still. It's okay." Canin kept repeating it over and over again and Hanlan finally relaxed.

"About time," the female voice said.

Hanlan was laying on his stomach and he could feel a hand resting on the back of his bare shoulder.

Now that he had calmed he could also feel a warmth shooting through that area along with the pain. "What happening?" he croaked out.

Canin stopped his repetition, then said, "She's rebuilding your shoulder. The bullet shattered your shoulder blade."

"Knew that," he croaked.

"The accelerated healing you got as my companion would have healed you with a shattered shoulder blade."

Hanlan thought of the consequences of that. He didn't like it. There seemed to be serious cons to this companion thing.

"There," the woman said as the hand withdrew from his shoulder and the bed moved. "He should rest tonight and don't move the arm as much as possible. Tomorrow he should be able to use it naturally."

"Thank you, Nodi," Canin said. "Will you give my regrets to the Alpha? I won't be attending the Hunt."

"Of course." There was some movement, then a hand laid over Hanlan's eyes. The woman muttered something Hanlan didn't catch, then the hand lifted. "Open your eyes, companion."

Hanlan blinked his eyes a few times, then kept them open and stared at the old woman in front of him.

She reminded him of his great grandmother with her gray hair in a bun at the back of her head. Her dress was homespun but her shaw was multi-colored. Hoop earrings hung from her ears and she wore a stone necklace. Cognac eyes met his briefly as she smiled toothily at him.

Canin sat on the floor next to the bed with concerned eyes.

Nodi picked up the glass on the nightstand and put the straw on Hanlan's lips. "It's just water," she said when Hanlan didn't drink.

Hanlan looked at Canin who nodded, then pulled the straw into his mouth and drank. The coolness relieved his sore throat, but he only took a few sips before pushing the straw out with his tongue.

Canin took the glass from Nodi and held it as she thrust it toward him.

"Get him to drink as much as possible and eat some of the soup," she told Canin as she turned away from the bed and began moving toward the door. "He needs to replenish his energy."

"Okay. Thanks again, Nodi."

She flash Canin a smile, then vanished out the door.

"Spill," Hanlan said hoarsely.

The bedroom was dim as only the lamp on the nightstand was on in the dark room and night had fallen outside so little light came from the tiny rectangular window on the one wall. Canin sat within the circle of light so Hanlan could see his face, and he now moved closer up so he could hold the straw to Hanlan's lips.

Hanlan took another drink, but it didn't distract him. "Well?"

"Where do you want me to start?"

"Who is Nodi?"

"One of the Pack's healers."

"You need healers? I thought your body healed

itself."

"For the most part. But if the trauma is too severe, then we require a healer's service. Also they are also our therapists. Healers keep the Pack healthy in more than one way."

"Why didn't you want it known I was injured?"

"The accelerated healing would have been noticeable to the EMT's and then the doctors. Also you would have been unconscious and whomever has your medical proxy would be in charge of your medical decisions. Then there's the shattered shoulder blade. It wouldn't have healed. There are limitations with the accelerated healing companions have," he finished sheepishly.

"Then we have a problem. I can't go without medical treatment all the time."

"Nodi and I can show you how to slow down the healing for a time with a minor wound, but major wounds brings on the restorative sleep." He gave Hanlan the straw again, then set the glass on the nightstand. "Think you can get up? Without using that arm?" he asked as he got to his feet.

"I'll try." Hanlan moved around until he was on his right side, then flopped onto his back. He reached up with his right hand and Canin grasped it to pull him upright. Keeping a grip on Canin, Hanlan spun his legs to the side and allowed Canin to draw him to his feet. Once he got his balance, he let go of his partner.

Canin grabbed something off the nightstand and held it out to Hanlan.

It was a sling. Hanlan took it and carefully put it on. After his arm was settled, he followed Canin out to the living room and into the kitchen. He sat at the table and watched as Canin went over to the stove where a soup pan was set. "What's that?"

"It's called ironically enough Gypsy Soup. Nodi brought it." He ladled up a bowl for Hanlan and set it before him. "It will help restore the energy you used up with both the accelerated healing and Nodi's healing." Canin retrieved a spoon and handed it to Hanlan. "Eat up."

Hanlan took the spoon but looked at Canin for a moment before digging into the soup. He was starving.

Canin got him a glass of water, then sat at the table next to him.

There was a lot Hanlan could say about what happened, but he could tell that Canin wouldn't listen nor did he himself want to talk about it so he left it lie. Except for one thing. "How did you explain it?"

"Sgt. Dan might be in league with Lowell and thought getting rid of us would slow down the pursuit."

Hanlan nodded, then looked at him. "You're writing the notes and report."

"Of course." Canin cracked a smile.

Finishing the soup, Hanlan then drank some of the water. He set the glass down and looked at Canin again. "What was that about a Hunt?"

"We have a—tradition, I guess you'd call it. On October 31, the last day of the Ruven year, we transform into our wolf forms and hunt. Usually as a pack, but sometimes singularly if we are alone."

"And the prey of this hunt?" Hanlan asked

cautiously.

"Chosen by the Alpha of the pack."

Hanlan notice Canin's tone was bland. He left this lie as well and changed to a different subject. "Ruven year?"

"The changing of the season to winter begins the Ruven year. We are told that while we adopted the names and timing of the months from our Chosen Roma we are to keep our own year and count."

"Count?"

"Yes, by the Ruven calendar it is 7743."

"7743?" He blinked, then asked, "How long do Ruv live?"

"Not that long. We're not immortal."

Hanlan just stared at him with a raised eyebrow.

"The oldest among us reached nine hundred and forty-eight."

A whistle passed Hanlan's lips at the number. True, no living thing was immortal, but that was close enough for him. "And you're..?"

"A little over two hundred." Canin stood and took Hanlan's bowl to the sink. He sat the dish in it, then turned to Hanlan. "You should go back to bed. Nodi said you need to rest."

Hanlan tiredly got to his feet and headed to the bedroom. He had a lot to think about and didn't reckon he'd get to sleep with his head buzzing. His house phone rang and he stopped in the bedroom doorway.

Canin motioned him on and picked up the phone himself.

Moving inside the room, he struggled to unbuckle his belt. He finally got it as he stood by the bed and he let it fall with the weight of his gun dragging it down. Taking off the sling, he sighed in relief, then stepping out of his pants he got onto the bed. Getting under the covers would be too much work and it was warm enough in the apartment so he just laid his body on top.

"That was the captain," Canin said as he entered. "She wants a report Monday morning." He was almost to the bed when he shimmered. His wolf form joined Hanlan on the bed, laying against his side.

Warmth, both mental and physical, crept over Hanlan and he found his mind quieting. Hopefully, the bloody dream wolves would stay away. Maybe all his nightmares would.

CHAPTER 28

Sunday morning was spent in bed. Hanlan hadn't woken up until Canin had brought him coffee and a breakfast burrito. After he had eaten, Hanlan had gingerly gotten dressed in casual clothes, then had went into the living room to collapse on the couch, still tired. And that was where he stayed.

Canin was in human form, sitting on a chair reading the Sunday paper. He had been there as long as Hanlan had been on the couch.

A knock sounded on Hanlan's back door.

Both of them tensed, then Canin got up and went to answer it.

The two people that returned with him made Hanlan straighten up.

Phuro stopped just inside the room, but Lupo walked over and settled in one of the chairs. The old Ruv frowned at her, then went to the chair by the couch and sat down, keeping himself between Hanlan and Lupo.

Canin sat on the couch next to Hanlan and didn't take his eyes off of Lupo.

They sat in silence for a while before Hanlan asked, "What do you want?"

Lupo raised an eyebrow.

"Why are you here?" Hanlan clarified.

"You two need to clear the air, so to speak," Phuro said.

Hanlan and Lupo looked at each other, then at Phuro. "Ain't happening," came from Hanlan and Lupo shook her head, saying "I told you this was a waste of time."

Phuro frowned.

"Her obsession pulls her into Shilmulo territory," Hanlan told him. "Killing the Graves isn't the only wrong thing she's done."

"They were dupes of the Hunters." Lupo said it as if that was a reason instead of an excuse. "The book wouldn't have been safe."

"It probably wouldn't have been found."

"You found it." She empathized the words as if he was something she had found on her shoe.

"Julia," Phuro said. His voice held a warning and she bowed her head briefly. "He is a companion and should be accorded the respect that deserves."

"He also has the Sight," Canin said, speaking up. "I trust his instincts."

"Both of you just stay out of my way." Lupo

stood and nodded to Phuro before heading toward the back door.

Canin followed after her, leaving Hanlan and Phuro alone.

"I see no signs of madness in her," Phuro said as if to excuse himself.

"Her obsession with Raven Manor as I said is what pulls her into the darkness. You or Canin will have to kill her one day." Phuro looked at him sharply but Hanlan kept his eyes on the doorway to the kitchen. "She will step over even your line."

Canin returned and settled on the couch next to Hanlan. "She's gone," he assured Hanlan.

Hanlan nodded and relaxed his body. He had been tense the whole time Lupo had been there. "Did you want to speak to us?" he asked Phuro as the older Ruv had made no move to leave after Lupo had left.

"To you. We are not having any luck with finding Oru. Can you give us something, anything to go on?"

"Perhaps they are meant to find you."

Phuro frowned at him again.

"What's happening with the Trust?" Canin asked before Phuro could say anything to Hanlan's comment.

"Deneque will probably instigate a missing person report tomorrow while Cowen fortifies her position. He's the favorite for the director's chair and there's no love loss between them. There will probably be an internal war. While that will be good for the Ruv as a whole, it will be bad for me. I'm in a tenuous position at the Trust. I had Carson's protection but with her gone, I'm at the mercy of Cowen and Deneque."

"They'd kill you?" Hanlan raised an eyebrow.

"Cowen would, but I think Deneque would be more subtle."

"A stalking horse."

"Yes." Phuro nodded.

"What about the book?" Hanlan asked. "Will it be safe if something happens to you?"

"Gayl is the only one besides us who knows the book is even there. It's safe."

Phuro hadn't really answered his question but Hanlan let it go. After all it wasn't his responsibility.

"Are you moving in here?" Phuro asked Canin.

Canin glanced at Hanlan before looking at the Ruv alpha. "We haven't discussed that yet."

"Perhaps you should." Phuro stood. "As the French would say Au Revoir," he told them as he headed toward the kitchen and the back door.

Canin hopped up and scurried after him.

Hanlan waited patiently for his return. He knew Canin was apprehensive, but he didn't need to be.

The Ruv entered tentatively and sat stiffly on the chair by the couch.

"These last few nights I've slept better than I have in a long time." He paused as he felt Canin's satisfaction. "You would be welcome to stay."

Happiness and excitement flared but Canin just said, "Thank you."

"I don't know what I'm going to tell the captain about all this." Hanlan changed the subject. He had enough of emotion for the time being. "Three females' obsession with Raven Manor caused all this havoc yet only one is going to get the blame for all of it."

"That's what you tell her. It's a case of obsession."

Hanlan rubbed his face, tiredly, then looked toward the kitchen. "Any of that soup left?"

"Yes." Canin jumped to his feet. "I'll get you some."

Canin disappeared into the kitchen and Hanlan slumped. Tomorrow he'd no doubt be back to his old self, well physically anyway. But right now he was tired, both mentally and physically. This case had taken a toll and brought about change to his once ordinary life.

Well, if you can call the life of a homicide detective ordinary.

A type of cold war had been going on between the Ruv and the Trust/Hunters under the noses of most humans. It could heat up, depending on what went on with the Trust, and there could be collateral damage in the form of dead bodies—human and Ruv.

Canin returned with a bowl and a glass and set them on the coffee table before going back into the kitchen.

Hanlan moved until he was sitting upright, then scooted forward to lean over the coffee table. He grabbed the universal remote and turned on the TV, muting it immediately as it blared. Hitting the sound button a few times, he lowered the sound before un-muting it. He wasn't really listening. It was just noise but he didn't like silence. Silence led to contemplation.

His partner came back with a cup of coffee.

"That better be for me," Hanlan told him.

"It is." Canin put it down next to the glass of water.

"Aren't you going to eat?" he asked when his partner sat in the chair by the couch instead of going back to the kitchen.

"I don't need to."

A light bulb went off in his head. Canin had drank Sgt. Dan's blood. Hanlan started to eat the soup, then stopped and looked at Canin. "Blood?"

"The elixir of life. We do not eat flesh as ghostwolves, though we can in human form."

"I have a lot to learn."

"And time to learn it."

Hanlan finished the soup and drank half a glass of water before settling back with his coffee. "Alright, give me Ghostwolves 101."

Canin laughed. "Tell me what your great grandmother told you first."

"Alright. She always started with—It was a dark and stormy night..."

EPILOGUE

Hanlan had spent that night telling Canin every Ruven and Shilmulo tale his great grandmother had ever uttered to him as a boy. He had remembered them as if she had just told them to him. But he never found out if they were true because he had fallen asleep still talking.

Canin had awoken him with coffee and a breakfast burrito. They'd have to go shopping if this continued. He hurriedly ate and dressed before they headed to the station.

When they got there, Jack Reach was in the evidence room. He gave them a thumbs up as they went toward the elevator and Hanlan sighed in relief. If Reach said it was okay, then the cover story had held up. He could run with that.

The captain was waiting when they entered the bullpen but Hanlan was no longer apprehensive. He glanced at Canin who sat down at his desk, then followed the captain to her office. Everything was good. He'd be able to go back to ordinary murders.

At least for now.

ABOUT THE AUTHOR

This is T.L.'s first in the Ghostwolf series. Ghostwolves or Del Mulanti Ruv live among us but do not mistake them for humans. These books are one companion's journey through their world.

To learn more about the Del Mulanti Ruv and upcoming books visit the author at her main blog. Https://tlriffey.blogspot.com or her website https://panthersprite.wixsite.com/sidereal

If you like this book, please leave a review. The author would love some feedback.

T.L. lives in Southern Missouri with a bevy of feral cats.